*A
Harlequin
Romance*

OTHER
Harlequin Romances
by JOYCE DINGWELL

Many of these titles are available at your local bookseller,
or through the Harlequin Reader Service.

For a free catalogue listing all available Harlequin Romances,
send your name and address to:

HARLEQUIN READER SERVICE,
M.P.O. Box 707, Niagara Falls, N.Y. 14302
Canadian address: Stratford, Ontario, Canada N5A 6W4

or use order coupon at back of books.

THE NEW BROOM

by

JOYCE DINGWELL

Harlequin Books

ORONTO • LONDON • NEW YORK • AMSTERDAM • SYDNEY • WINNIPEG

Original hardcover edition published in 1974
by Mills & Boon Limited

ISBN 0-373-01981-5

Harlequin edition published June, 1976

Printed in Canada

CHAPTER ONE

Sophie. Feeling like Christmas and it was only July. Dancing down the school corridor to the office marked "Headmistress" with the sparkling knowledge that it would soon have to be corrected to "Headmaster." Knowing it would be Father at the top and not Father's Wife.

She had called Honor that: Father's Wife. Honor had not minded at all, in fact she had suggested it. "You wouldn't want to call me Mother, Sophie, and in front of the other teachers it can scarcely be Honor. Just address your father as Father as usual and me as Father's Wife."

She had been a wonderful women, and a perfect step-parent, and Sophie had appreciated her, appreciated the tact, wit and intelligence that had got her where she was . . . also where Father had insisted she remain.

"Because we are being married, Honor, there's no reason you should resign," he had said. "No one knows better than another teacher how hard it is to win those gold letters on the door."

As strictly only a Craft and Manual master himself he had known his own chances of prinicipal at any college had been distinctly remote, that that head position belonged traditionally to Arts, Science or Maths graduates. (Honor had been a History M.A.) But Sophie had just learned the stunning news that Father, though through no trying of his own, had beaten tradition. He was to be the first headmaster ever of the Apa School for Girls.

The post-office had pointed it out when Sophie had collected the school mail from the village. "Headmaster now," Miss Watts had commented of a large official letter, "so your father is not Mr. Headmistress any more." She had spoken affectionately.

From the day he had married Honor, for some young-girl reason the pupils had addressed Father as Mr. Headmistress instead of Sir or Mr. Arthur, and the staff, and, indeed, all the village, had followed suit. Because he was lovable and much loved they had known he would not object. He hadn't, but deep down his daughter Sophie had. She had liked Honor tremendously, but she had longed for Father . . . just once . . . to come first.

Well, it had happened. "Headmaster now," Miss Watts had said, and had proved it with the official mail. For the three months since Honor had died, and Father had substituted, the mail had come addressed : "Acting Director." Now it was : "Headmaster." So Father was the Principal of the Apa School for Girls.

Apa was aboriginal for water, and the college was aptly named. There was water everywhere. In the far distance the Pacific Ocean rolled smoothly into the fabulous beaches of south-east Queensland, then came the man-made quays and canals of Surfers' Paradise served by its shining Nerang River, then finally here, in the hinterland, and at the foot of Apa School on Apa Mountain, there were so many waterfalls, pools, cascades and streams that when Sophie took out the nature class it was hard to keep dry. It was breathtakingly beautiful, from the shouting blue of the coast to the aching green valleys with their stands of ten-thousand-year-old Zamia palms and ancient fig trees, and even the practical parents looking for a good

6

education for their daughters, or good food, or good air, had stopped being practical for a moment to stare out instead and say:

"Well, Mary . . . Jean . . . Alice should be happy here."

As far back as Sophie could remember they had been happy, due as well as to those other things to Honor and her husband, to Headmistress and Mr. Headmistress. Now they would be just as happy, she knew, with Headmaster on top at last. Dear Father, the Headmaster. Sophie turned the handle of the door.

A man was seated at the desk, but he was not Father, even though he sat in Father's, late Honor's, chair. It annoyed Sophie, but she supposed the parent, for he would be that, had been invited to sit down and had simply sat. Father must have been called out, possibly to hear the stunning news that she had just heard, for he was not here. With a little sigh, for she felt more like skating than being quietly solicitous to a new parent, Sophie came and sat down where the visitor should rightly have sat.

"Good morning, Mr——?" she began.

"Good morning," the man returned uncompromisingly.

His deliberate lack of co-operation nettled Sophie. However, he might be cloaking his emotion by abruptness. Honor had taught her that. "Sometimes," Honor had related, "they are downright rude, but I know it's only because instead of a parent they are about to become an absent parent." Dear wise Honor! Sophie recalled her strategies, and borrowed them now.

"Your child will be in safe hands, Mr——?" she tried again, yet again he did not tell her. But he did correct her with:

"Children, not child."

"Really. How nice," Sophie said.

She found the attendance book, opened it and confirmed the fact that Father had not entered the new ones up as yet.

"Kindergarten, junior or senior section?" she asked kindly.

"What do you think?" he came back.

It was an odd answer, but Honor had warned that most parents, particularly the male variety, do and say odd things.

She looked at him estimatingly. Definitely not old yet certainly not young. His daughters, she decided, could be about— She tried:

"Elementary junior and advanced junior," was not corrected, so she found the appropriate page. "Names?" she inquired next.

He shrugged and suggested that she try once more; it was a silly answer, but she still must keep in mind what Honor had said about Parents: Peculiarities of.

"I think Janet and Louise," she guessed, and he gave a non-committal nod.

She wrote down Janet, left a space, then Louise and left a space, congratulating herself on being very clever—or lucky, though really this was the most ridiculous enrolment she had ever done. She wished her father would return.

"Blue curriculum or gold?" she queried. "Blue is academic, gold embraces domestic subjects and crafts."

"Take your pick," he said.

"Really, Mr—" Sophie controlled herself and smiled perfunctorily. "I mean perhaps we should wait until we find out the girls' natural inclinations.—Any weaknesses I can pass on to Matron? Like spring colds or an inability to drink milk?" She said the last a little indistinctly. Without a doubt he was the most uncooperative parent she had ever encountered.

He still did not co-operate, so she went on: "Then swimming. Can they, or can't they? We take the can'ts in our mini-bus down to the surf, for the natural mountain clefts here are sometimes dangerously deep and always very cool, and we have no installed pool."

"I don't know," he said.

"Don't know?" She stared at him, then reminded herself of Parents, and tried again.

"Vacations. You take them home for vacations?"

"My God, no. Perish the thought!"

"I beg your pardon?"

"You heard," he said.

"I thought I did, but—"

"I said 'My God, no,' and I meant it. Not a hundred and fifty of them."

"A hundred and fifty! But that would be the entire school."

"Exactly."

"And you certainly couldn't do that."

"I just said so."

"I don't think I quite understand you, Mr—?"

"Perhaps not, but I believe I am beginning to understand you. You're on the staff here?"

"I'm the gym teacher, and when phys ed is not required I double up with nature study lessons." Sophie paused. "The former, the phys ed, I mean, is compulsory, I'm afraid."

"Why are you afraid?"

Sophie was beginning to get impatient, to forget all that Father's Wife had advised her.

"Because it's very apparent you're not at all impressed with me, but for all your pre-distrust your child . . . children . . . will still have to have me, since gym work and physical exercises are compulsory, Mr. . . . what was the name again?"

"It was not again. But *your* name, please?"

"Why should I give it if you withhold yours?"

"A very good reason, surely." He gave her a thin, significant smile, at least she took it as significant, and guessed why.

"You mean a teacher should be polite to a prospective parent?" she conceded unwillingly. "Very well. I'm Miss Arthur."

"Oh, I see." A pause. "Daughter of Mr. Arthur."

"Daughter of the Headmaster," she said proudly, and waited for his impressed capitulation.

It did not come. Instead one word came, one word only.

"No."

"Sir?"

"Saxby." Quite unmistakably *he* waited now, waited for her reaction to that, but, the same as with his capitulation that had not eventuated, Sophie's reaction was nil.

There was a moment of silence. On the wall the hand of the big clock moved up another minute. Then:

"Saxby, B.A., BEc. B.Sc., Hon, Syd. Uni," he said, and he actually pronounced the initials, though if it was done humorously, Sophie found nothing to laugh at. Then he said, and no initials now, the full works:

"Headmaster of Apa." He waited, then added: "For boys and girls."

She had been dumbfounded, but that "boys" discovered her tongue again.

"Ah, you're at the wrong school. We're girls only."

"Correction, please. You were."

"But—"

"At the last board meeting it was decided to do what most schools now are doing, go co-ed."

"Co-ed? Apa co-ed?" Sophie gasped.

"In which case it was deemed better to have a headmistress no longer, so. . . ." He gave a slight and ironic

10

bow.

"But—but my father—"

"Yes? Your father?"

"All these months he's been deputy. Even when Honor was principal he was Mr. Headmistress."

"I beg your pardon, Miss Arthur?"

"It was something the girls called him, and Father didn't mind at all." Sophie suddenly felt a little silly.

The man who *said* he was the headmaster nodded. "And you, being the daughter, became Miss Headmistress, I presume? Though dreaming, no doubt, of being Miss Headmaster one day."

She ignored that. She said: "I can't believe it."

"Then kindly begin at once."

"Does . . . does Father know?"

"Ask him yourself, Miss Arthur, he has gone out to bring me up some pottery his classes have been doing."

"Yes, he takes the Craft and Manual lessons," Sophie murmured. Suddenly to her annoyance she felt her face crumpling, her eyes beginning to smart with tears. "Poor dear," she burst out.

"I rather think you mean poor dear's dear," the man suggested laconically, noticeably unmoved by the break in her voice. "For someone pipped at the post and merely retaining his old post, Mr. Arthur seemed to me to be a very contented person."

" . . . Contented? I'm as happy as I've been for months, since before Honor went, in fact. You can keep executive work." Occupied in herself, in the news, in the man opposite, Sophie had not seen her father come back into the room.

"This is it, Garrick" . . . Garrick? . . . "turn it round, tilt it, catch the light." Father demonstrated the urn he had carried in. "Actually every dye used was won out of the bush here. We're all very proud of that fact." He became aware of Sophie, and put on an official expression. "I see you've met my daughter, Mr. Saxby," he bowed. "Sophie, meet the headmaster."

"Madam," acknowledged the man, and Sophie mumbled something in reply. It could have been "How are you, Mr. Saxby," or it could have been something else, anything else. All she knew it was *not* Headmaster. Not . . . and never . . . that.

Yet he was indeed Headmaster. It was discussed in the staff room over tea. The thing that was not discussed, and it inflamed Sophie, was the gross unfairness of it. No one seemed at all surprised that Father had been passed over.

All the staff members were female, and Sophie came in when she got the chance with an astringent remark that it was rather an effeminate post for a youngish man. For Father it would have been different, he was oldish. This man Saxby was not.

"Not effeminate for the principal of a co-ed, Sophie," they disagreed.

"Small prep boys," Sophie sniffed. Most of the girls' colleges accepted young male preps; it had been considered once, yet never carried out, at Apa.

"No, *not* small preppers, the usual school age, seven to seventeen."

Sophie had no answer to that.

She listened to them anticipating other male additions to the staff, appropriate teachers for the boys' curriculum : instructors in mechanics, tech drawing, architecture, and, of course, male variety phys ed. They supposed aloud that Sophie would be kept strictly to eurythmics and dancing for the girls.

"It will be like a new school," they enthused, and they sounded lit up, stimulated.

Sophie got up, she felt choked. Murmuring something about seeing to her new bulbs, she went out. It did not help that not one of the absorbed staff noticed her go.

It was a lovely garden, flamboyant as are most Queensland gardens, with their scarlet poinsettias, rich red crotons, huge hibiscus, creamy frangipanni, and orchids growing free. Because contrarily one always wants what one can't have, Sophie had sent away to Melbourne for some cool climate corms and tried to coax up a bed of lachenalia. They certainly had risen from the earth, but there they had stopped, a miserable little row of expatriates from the south.

"Meaning you should be content with your lot, bloom in your own plot." Father had joined Sophie.

She looked at him covertly. Certainly if he was disappointed, he was not showing it. For a man who had been pipped at the post as—Garrick, wasn't it?—Saxby had said, he did not seem at all downcast. But then Father had always been a very controlled man. Sophie's own mother, Margaret, had been his dear love, yet when she had left him there had been no outward sign of his deep loss. Honor, too. Sophie had been very aware of his deep regard for his second wife, yet he had still remained the same calm man.

Life had not been fair to him, she thought resentfully. He had come up north to teach because Sophie had been a young schoolgirl and this school would accept his daughter as well as him. Another man would have chaffed a little in the all-female company, but if Father had, he had hidden it with a smile. He had stayed on, endearing himself to everybody . . . and especially, as it had turned out, to the Head. When Sophie had reached leaving age, Honor had spoken to the Board and they had retained Sophie as phys ed teacher with a nature study class here and there when there were periods to be filled in. Then

Honor and Father had married. It had been an excellent arrangement for all, though now Sophie had her doubts. Perhaps it would have been better if they had not married after all, if she, Sophie, had gone away and become a clerk somewhere, for undoubtedly Father, with his dead Margaret's injunctions still in his mind, would have come, too, even though he had to leave Honor. Father and daughter would have found a new flat, new jobs, but—grimly—never a job like this one for Father, a post promising things that did not eventuate, only yielded after years of devoted work a cruel letdown.

"Sophie, I'm speaking to you," Father said, sounding anything but cruelly let down.

"Yes. About the lachenalia."

"About blossoming in your own plot, Sophie."

"Oh, Father, why didn't *you*? Why have they rewarded you with this?" She cupped her hands as though holding in them the smaller secondary job that he still only retained.

He looked at her ruefully. He could have explained everything in a few telling words, but no, not to his Sophie.

"My dear, if you're speaking of the headmastership—"

"Of course I am!"

"A head with only a Craft and Manual diploma, my Sophie!"

"Perhaps not in Sydney," Sophie conceded, "Melbourne, any of those places, but this is—well, a country corner."

"And a very good school."

"But after all those months of being deputy . . ."

"I was pleased and proud to stand in, it was what Honor wanted."

"You mean—"

"Yes, I do mean that, Sophie. Honor *asked* me to do it."

"But she didn't ask you to—to continue in her role?"

He hesitated. Again he thought how a few words would answer everything, but again he asked himself how could he? To Sophie?

"She didn't," deduced Sophie in a low voice. She felt disappointed in Honor.

"Perhaps I could have managed a bunch of girls," Father said presently and humorously, or at least Sophie supposed he tried for humour, "but never a bunch of boys."

"Is that co-ed business really true?" Sophie asked.

"Yes, it is true."

"It's a wonder some of my girls with applicable brothers haven't heard the news and told me, then," Sophie still doubted.

"There were no vacancies," Mr. Arthur explained, "so it was not made public. You remember the cliff school down at Kingsley on the coast?"

"Academy for Boys," nodded Sophie.

"Well, it isn't any longer, neither Kingsley, neither on the cliff, nor for boys. It's moved, or about to be moved, to Apa Mountain, and to become co-ed. A high-rise is taking its place by the sea, and we're taking Kingsley into our own natural high-rise Apa." He laughed, but once again Sophie could not join in.

"It seems to me that everything is having to have something else to take its place," she commented tartly.

"Sophie, thank heaven you're phys ed and not English! I'm not inanimate. Nor is Mr. Saxby."

"Garrick," Sophie murmured.

"But on that subject, Sophie, the subject of phys ed and occasional nature study classes, you do realize, of course, that you are now more or less on—well, approbation?"

"What, Father?"

"Honor *found* a place for you, she *created* it, you were never actually qualified."

"I'm sure there was never any need for the school board to have any regrets."

"That's not the point, Sophie. Now that the school is expanding, it's only natural that its demands will be expanding as well. Where you fitted the bill nicely before, now it will be up to what the headmaster requires and thinks."

"And does," finished Sophie. She considered the prospect and did not like it. To be dependent, she writhed, on *him*.

"Father, it's so rottenly unfair," she burst out. "For you. For me."

"I think you've been treated very fairly, dear, considering your lack of any diploma."

"But if I'd known this lay ahead—"

"Oh, come, child, you haven't been dismissed. Not yet, anyway." He smiled again.

"Nor you," Sophie said cryptically. "How long before *you* will be going, Mr. Arthur? How long before you leave Apa?"

He did not answer her at once. Once again he was thoughtful as though he wished to say something. But when he spoke it was placatingly again.

"We're talking nonsense, of course. I get on very well with Garrick."

"Garrick already?"

"Yes, dear. Sophie, I want you to get on with him as well."

"I—and all the staff," she despaired. "You should see them, Father, absolutely featherbrained over the appearance of a male. At least" . . . apologetically . . . "another male."

"You mean a more contemporary one. Well, that's only natural. Sophie, promise me."

"Promise what?"

"Not to antagonize Garrick Saxby. After all——"

"After all, I'm on approval," she nodded.

"After all, he doesn't have to have you, my dear."

"Neither did Father's Wife have to have me."

"That was quite different."

"I suppose so." Sophie shrugged. "But does it matter so much, Father? If I'm not suitable . . . you, too, who knows? . . . can't we simply leave and start somewhere else?"

"No," Mr. Arthur said quickly, and Sophie looked curiously at him, surprised at the decision in his answer.

He was glancing away, obviously a little embarrassed at his own fervour.

"Because of Honor?" Sophie said sympathetically. That would be it, he would not want to leave his fond memories of Honor.

"Yes. Yes, dear. Honor." He said it almost with relief.

She squeezed his arm, and as she did it she thought with surprise how frail he suddenly seemed.

"Father, are you all right?"

"Of course I am. Not up to your physical jerks perhaps, but quite fit for my age."

"It's the last months, I expect," Sophie nodded, "they must have been a strain. And to think after all that worry——"

"If you're going to start that headmastership all over again, Sophie, then I'd sooner you do it on your own." Father turned.

He seemed older somehow, a little smaller, more stooped . . . a kind of going downhill look.

Sophie ran after him. "I'll be good."

He knew she meant Garrick Saxby, and he smiled back at her.

"Thank you, daughter." He crinkled his eyes at her, an old sign between them, and went back to the school.

Sophie weeded the lachenalia, though she knew it would make no difference. As she worked, she pondered. If staying meant all that to Father, she thought, then she would go along with him.

All the same, it would be hard.

Honor's suite had been in the best position of all Apa, as befitted a headmistress. And now as befitted a headmaster? Sophie asked herself this as she went into the more privileged apartment some time later.

She crossed as usual to the picture window to stare out, she never grew tired of looking down on the amazing vistas of Surfers' Paradise. Her eyes reluctantly left their own lush green valley beneath Apa Mountain, with its crystal streams, its palms and wild limes dressed up with vines and orchids and gemlike parrots, to take in the crumpled blue-green carpets of foothills, then the smooth flats that extended to the ocean. In some cases the flats had been turned into quays and canals, and from up here the development looked like a shining mosaic. Sophie frequently marvelled at what man can do; one week there would be nothing but ugly heaps of clay and mud and ooze, the next week the scene would be a row of gay waterside villas, all with their own bright jetties and marinas. The high-rises, too, instead of being concrete edifices became tall poppies from Apa. Sophie did not dislike them, not, anyway, from the distance of the mountain. During the day they loomed dreamlike and unreal in the faintly blue coastal air, and at night they tried to outdo the moon rising out of the Pacific with their electric glitter, or they reached even further up to borrow a diadem of stars to wear on top of one of their many penthouses.

Yes, it was all beautiful from the VIP suite, and she would miss it.

Sophie turned back again.

Before Father had married Honor, the Arthurs had occupied the western rooms. When they had moved into the VIP suite there had been no takers for their old flat. The other teachers were already comfortably settled and had no desire to move, and no new staff had come in. But with the expected intake now there should be several needing accommodation, so Sophie decided, seeing their VIP days were over, to get cracking and claim the old residence again. It had no view like this, but at least it was self-contained and fairly roomy.

She gathered up an armful of things, went down the corridor and along to their previous rooms. Rather to her surprise, since the rooms apart from basic furniture had been left empty, the door was locked. She trudged back, deposited her bundle, then found their VIP key. Probably it would fit. Probably all the keys in Apa fitted. She went back, but still had no success.

She stood nibbling on her bottom lip. After that brief interlude with Mr. Garrick Saxby she wanted to be out of where she did not belong at once. But the thing was she did not want to search the Head out ... Head! ... and ask for the key. Suddenly she remembered the servery. It had never been used, and no one knew why it had ever been included at all when meals were taken in the school dining room, but now it offered Sophie a way out. Or at least a way in, she grinned. She found the aperture, decided entry would be a pushover, but took the precaution of going back first and changing into a more appropriate gym dress in case of any impeding corners. As always she sighed as she got into the gym dress. Honor, very outgoing in most things, had been inturned when it came to gym dresses for the instructress. No mod brief shorts and shirt for Sophie, but a pleated pinafore with a sailor blouse and knickers underneath, almost only a larger replica of the regulation school uniform (smaller if a student was ample.) Sophie tied back her shoulder-length hair to keep it from catching when she did her entry bit, then went down the corridor again.

There was no one around, and not likely to be anyone, as the hall led only to the empty flat. Without much difficulty Sophie scraped through the hole in the wall. She had barely got to her feet again when she saw that in one thing she had been very wrong. It was not an empty flat. A paper was flung down. A decanter was on the table, a coat laid over the back of a chair. And someone was in the bathroom.

A voice was raised in robust bathroom song, and it would have to be *his* voice, Garrick Saxby's tone, for it was a man's deeper range, and, apart from Father, the new headmaster was the only man here. The several gardeners and janitors never came into the house.

Sophie was taken completely by surprise. It had never occurred to her to wonder where Mr. Saxby would be sleeping, if it had she would have thought vaguely of some hotel down at Surfers' Paradise until he moved into the Apa VIP suite.

Congratulating herself that she had not roused him, she tiptoed to the door. Here another surprise awaited her, an even more disagreeable one. The door was as locked this side as it had been on the outside, which was only to be expected, but what Sophie had not expected was no key in the keyhole. He must have carried the key with him into the bath. Well, there was

20

nothing for it than to go back the way she had come in. Sophie once more inserted her head and shoulders.

The corridor was clear, so she heaved herself through the aperture . . . or at least that was the idea. But it didn't turn out like that, not this time; where before she had had a fairly easy transit, either she approached it differently, or the passage through was constructed at an opposed angle when it was out from in instead of in from out, for, after getting as far as her waist, Sophie stuck.

She wriggled, she drew in deep breaths, she forced, she heaved, she even tried to get back into the room with the idea of trying the window instead, but every movement wedged her firmer still.

No longer caring if anyone saw her, so long as *he* did not see her, she called along the corridor for help, hoping her voice did not penetrate backwards, which could happen, since no longer could she hear his own baritone in the bath.

Then she knew *why* she wasn't hearing it. It was because he was no longer in the bath. Quite distinctly she could hear the padding footfalls that bare feet make, then an exclamation of surprise. After that there was nothing again, but it did not need Sophie's imagination to tell her that Garrick Saxby had hurriedly gone back for a gown.

She knew he had returned when she felt the pressure on her feet. He must be experienced in removing bodies from serveries, for he did not tug willy-nilly, he shoved, manipulated, turned, rolled, and then she was out. Out very unceremoniously. She landed on the floor. There, humiliated, Sophie would still have sat, only he caught the ponytail she had made of her hair and literally hauled her up by it.

"I don't know how girls are disciplined," he said, "my only experience is with boys, but, by heaven, I

21

know what I'd like to do to . . ." His voice stopped. Sophie knew why.

"I'm sorry, Mr. Saxby," she said.

"What in tarnation are you doing in my flat, Miss Arthur?"

"I didn't know it was yours. I thought yours would be ours. That's why I came to yours." She stopped, not out of breath from talking but from his irritated shaking of her.

"Make sense," he ordered.

"It used to be ours," she explained.

"This flat?"

"Until Father became Mr. Headmistress." She bit her lip.

"Whereupon you moved up to the presidential suite."

"The VIP rooms. Yes."

"So why are you here?"

"I was moving us back here."

"Through the hatch?"

"The door was locked."

"A habit of mine," he said laconically, "when I take a bath." At her quick glance, he added: "Yes, I'm still in my robe. Wait here, Miss Arthur, while I dress, it wouldn't look good if someone came in."

"How could they?" she asked tartly.

"Through the servery, perhaps," he tossed. "However, don't think I'm unlocking the door yet—you would only escape, and I have a few things for you to hear."

Sophie had nothing else to do but agree, she had no wish to be stuck again, so she duly waited. He did not take long. He came out in grey flannels and white open-necked shirt. He crossed to the decanter and poured two drinks. One . . . the one he handed her . . . he only put a small amount in and filled with

22

ginger ale. It annoyed Sophie. As it happened she liked it like that, but she saw no reason why he should take it for granted that she did not drink a stronger brew as he did. He must have read her thoughts. "You're under drinking age," he informed her.

"I'm—"

"I know how old in years," he forestalled her. "I looked it up. I looked up all the staff."

Sophie giggled at that, there were several on the staff who would not be pleased.

He stopped her laughter with his following words. "Also," he added, "I looked up qualifications." He stared hard at her.

"I think you're leading up to say 'Which you have not'," Sophie suggested.

"Yes, I was leading up to that. And you with your eye on being Miss Headmaster!"

There was silence for a few moments. How could she tell this absolutely unapproachable man that she had been only thinking of Father? Sophie rankled. Success, she thought bitterly, would have come easily to Garrick Saxby, she knew his smooth, self-assured, confident, ascendant type. She had met men like him, men who would have no idea of how it felt always to be next best. She would have given anything to have turned now and gone to the door, demand that he open it, inform him as he did so that she and Father would be leaving at once, that he could move into the VIP suite. Then she thought of Father, heard again the anxiety in his voice when she had suggested that they leave Apa.

"No," Father had said with every fibre of him.

"No." She realized she was repeating it aloud.

"Not with your eyes on Miss Headmaster?" he taunted. "You could have fooled me."

"I don't think anyone does that, Mr. Saxby."

"I try to see to it that they don't," he agreed. He looked around him. "Returning to the subject of your presence here, Miss Arthur, you tell me you climbed through the hatch to see the lie of the ground."

"I know it. Father and I lived here. No, I came to open the door to make the carrying of our things easier, but the door was locked, so I scrambled through instead."

"But couldn't scramble out," he nodded. "But why would you do such a thing as move before I told you?"

"I didn't want to be told," she answered frankly.

"Fair enough." He actually grinned.

"Can I move in now? Then I'll fix our suite . . . *yours* . . . for you."

"No."

"No, Mr. Saxby?"

"I'm not moving from here."

"It's a superior apartment."

"This is quite sufficient."

"The other is more suitable for a head." She gulped as she said that 'head' and she saw that he noticed, for he grinned again.

"Hard, isn't it?" he sympathized falsely. "A pretty big pill to swallow." As she did not answer, he resumed: "I will not be moving, not yet, anyway." His glance flicked to a small table by the window, and on the table was a photograph of a girl. She was a very lovely girl.

"I see," said Sophie. His fiancée, she thought. He would leave the move until he married, and then let his wife redecorate. They usually did that. Well, it would be nice to have Honor's apartment for a further period.

Then she heard him start to speak again, and thought wryly that that further period might be very brief indeed. For:

"I'm strictly a qualifications man, Miss Arthur, ordinarily I wouldn't countenance an uncertificated teacher on my staff."

"You mean I'll only be accepted now because of the expanding school," she said, forgetting for the moment that the new intake would be strictly male, and that women do not instruct young males in physical education.

He looked at her sharply to see if she was being funny, then he ran the tip of his tongue round the rim of his long, rather enigmatical mouth and said off-handedly: "Perhaps. Anyway, you're to remain."

"Thank you."

"Also, for the present, anyway, remain in the front suite."

"Thank you."

"Very well then, Miss Arthur, seeing you have no further need to reconnoitre perhaps you will depart."

"Yes. I'm sorry." Sophie turned and went out.

It was not until she was back in the best suite that she realized she had said a very ridiculous thing, she had assumed she would be retained because of the bigger school, and he had answered just as ridiculously: "Yes."

A eurythmics and dancing teacher . . . or so the staff had said . . . for a bunch of future front row forwards!

Sophie could have laughed over it had she not been puzzled as to *why* he had agreed with her.

There's something else here, she thought, there must be something else, but apart from the ordinary and ever-present staff shortage that schools suffer, she could think of no other reason.

She remembered basketball practice for the third grades, and, already suitably clad in her gym dress,

25

ran down to the courts.

Dinner was at six-thirty. The staff ate in an inner room and the school in the big hall that led into the staff annexe. Teachers were rostered to dine with the girls at table, but tonight was not Sophie's night, so she went through to the annexe, wondering where she and Father would now sit. Since Honor had gone, Father had been occupying the Head's chair.

She was just in time to see a little tableau. It was Father graciously indicating the head position to Garrick Saxby and Mr. Saxby bowing just as graciously and accepting it. Why not, it was easy to be gracious when you were on top. But something in the way the men's eyes met and held held Sophie. She stood looking, until Miss Prentice, behind her, said: "Please, Sophie, you're holding everything up." Miss Prentice was obviously eager to be seated, as was everyone else. All eyes were on the new headmaster. Anyone would think, Sophie writhed, they had been man-starved.

Mr. Saxby included them all in the ensuing conversation, which centred naturally enough around the new scheme. He asked for questions, and they came from all the teachers except Sophie. If the head noticed this he gave no sign. He took query after query and answered it patiently, fully and confidentially. He just had to win with that confidential bit, rankled Sophie.

She listened to Marion Javes asking about future meals once the co-ed system commenced. They would all be eating together, and that included the staff, he replied. The dividing wall of the annexe would be knocked down to make an even larger large hall, large enough to seat the entire school, boys, girls, teachers.

"Boys and girls all over again," trilled Jane Ferris

of the teachers. She giggled.

"That's quite true, Miss Ferris," said Mr. Saxby. "Besides the Kingsley boys we will be accepting the Kingsley male staff."

There was an air of excitement. Everyone seemed to have had a shot in the arm, thought Sophie dismayed. Even the children were pepped up, the older ones looking sheep-eyed already . . . Sophie's description . . . and the younger ones plotting to take the boys for a few rides. Again Sophie's expression.

"I know a boy at Kingsley, he's Roger Werris. When he comes and when he's not looking I'm going to push him in the valley pool." It was Ariadne, a handful even among girls, so goodness only knew what she would be among boys.

Her shrill young voice had carried, and Sophie watched as Garrick Saxby put down his knife and fork to challenge through the door of the staff dining room:

"You do just that, Ariadne" . . . how could he know her name so soon? . . . "because Roger is a first-class swimmer and would enjoy it. But how about you when he does it back? Because you know what's done to others will certainly be done to you. I always make it a school rule."

"I can't swim," called Ariadne in panic.

"Then think it over." Garrick Saxby turned to the staff and said in a lower voice: "Not true, of course, she must be able to swim."

Everyone looked to Sophie, the p.e. mistress. (Sophie added dolefully to herself: 'But no diploma.')

"Miss Arthur?" Saxby asked.

"No, not all of them swim. I told you so when you enrolled your children . . . I mean I mentioned to you that I took the non-swimmers down to the coast to the surf." Sophie knew by her burning cheeks that she was flushing madly. "The mountain pools are only safe if you swim already," she mumbled.

"Presumably," he agreed drily. "And are they progressing?"

"Progressing?"

"With the swimming?"

"Well—it's difficult with surf."

"Especially when they build sandcastles instead."

Everyone laughed. You would have thought they had flagons of sparkling wine with their beef and veg, not carafes of water, Sophie thought angrily, they were practically intoxicated. But her anger was not against them—after all, they were only human and female, but against *him*. How had he known about the sandcastles? He must have seen her. The idea of his watching her as she raced around Mermaid Beach encouraging small shell collectors and junior jellyfish gatherers to try a few swimming strokes instead made her feel more foolish than she always felt down there. The surf was *not* the place for instruction, and Sophie had long since given the project up, and put it down as a day of sun and fresh air instead, so really not a loss after all.

"No," Garrick Saxby was saying, "not all of them can swim, but they will soon. We're having an Olympic standard pool installed at once, with a separate shallower one for the nervous beginners. However, that takes time. I would like as many pupils possible to swim before that time. We will look into things tomorrow, Miss Arthur. I think there must be a more suitable corner somewhere in the Paradise for teaching than the corner you have now."

"And what corner is that?" Sophie heard herself asking sharply. She still had that vision of his spying on her running up and down.

"The corner that evidently does not produce any

swimmers," he returned blandly. "Ladies, are you finished? Mr. Arthur, would you care to take your coffee with me?"

"And what goes with it," winked Olga Jessopp, going out with Sophie. "I must say it's good to see gracious living being practised again."

"You sound as though we've been living like savages."

"How touchy you are tonight, Sophie, I'm sure your father is enjoying his brandy with the coffee."

He might be finding enjoyment, thought Sophie, but I'm not, neither in brandy, nor in the change that has been brought about.

She went to the flat. She was not on duty at all this evening, neither in the homework room, the library or helping Matron in the bathrooms. She went to the window again.

The moon was rising out of the sea. The distant high-rises were putting on their lights, the penthouses borrowing the first stars to pin on their topmost roofs. Down below in the green valley there was only a velvety darkness, just black nothingness.

She would miss the Paradise and its hinterland abominably if she went away, but how could she possibly stay on now? Surely Father would agree when he saw his daughter's discontent, when she pointed out to him that for all his outward affability the new man was really patronizing Alex Arthur, that as soon as he got established and no longer needed the deputy head, the deputy head would go.

"Sitting in the dark, dear?" Father came into the flat, switching on as he entered.

"Yes. I've been thinking. Father——"

"Yes, Sophie?"

But Sophie did not go on. She had just received a shock, the shock of Father's distinct frailness. She had noticed it earlier today, but now it was much more noticeable. In the sudden bright electric light he looked all at once a tired, worn-out old man.

"Yes, Sophie?" he asked again.

"Are—are you glad we're not moving out of Honor's suite?" she changed.

"Garrick's now, dear. I thought that was very decent of him."

"But then he's a decent man," she said glibly.

"Yes, he is."

They looked across the hall at each other, the father, the daughter. Both wanted to speak, but neither did. Presently Mr. Arthur went into his study, and presently Sophie went to her bedroom. She heard lights out being sounded for the girls, and mechanically put out her own light, just as though she still was what *he* had taken her for this afternoon in her short gym dress. Still a schoolgirl.

Only I'm not, Mr. Garrick Saxby, Sophie said to the darkness; I don't know why you're keeping me on, unless it's your wish to keep Father for a while and take it that we both come in the one parcel, but it had better be good for my darling deputy or you'll know all about it from his daughter.

She heard laughter downstairs, a man's deeper timbre among the higher female timbre.

Mr. Garrick Saxby, Sophie thought, amusing his female underlings. But, shutting her eyes and shutting him out, he won't ever amuse me.

CHAPTER TWO

Sophie was rostered for breakfast duty the following morning, and although it was a chore she usually disliked, young females being as difficult and temperamental as their older sisters in the early morning, today she welcomed the task. From the staff dining room she could hear *his* voice, and if she had been present he would have seen her, would have recalled what he had planned for today. Now, with luck, he might forget.—With luck? Sophie accepted a folded note from Marcia Rossiter who had just passed the staff door and evidently been handed the message with an instruction to deliver it. Marcia said importantly: "He sent it."

"Not he, dear."—It was from Garrick Saxby, Sophie saw.

Above the scrawled signature Sophie read:

"Checking the timetables just now I see you have a non-swimmers' swim class this morning. Instead of depriving them, you will proceed as usual, and I will come also in the hope of finding some better learning location." Then came:

"Garrick Saxby."

He would, thought Sophie, he just would!

She stopped Veronique from pushing her eggs on to Andrea's plate. Veronique was reed slim and needed building up, while Andrea was far too plump and far too acquisitive foodwise. She reprimanded Betsy for trying to eat with her knife in her left hand and her

31

fork in her right for a change, Janice for emptying the entire sugar bowl on to her cereal. The first meal of the day was an important one, Honor had always maintained, and for this reason no interesting conversation was ever introduced, no advanced etiquette nicety, or "Can I have" in German or French. The girls were there strictly to begin their day with a good balanced intake, and Sophie tried to keep only that in mind. *Tried*, since it did not come instinctively as usual, since she had something else on her own plate. The swimming class . . . *and him* . . . she writhed.

"I don't like this jam, either," said Helen sympathetically.

"I do like it, Helen."

"Your face said Yuk," Helen insisted.

Sophie pulled herself together. She ran her mind over the non-swimmers, over the mini-busload of them, over what they always wore to the beach, for undoubtedly *he* would be watching with a critical eye this morning.

Lenore, for instance, crowed it over the others in a far too sophisticated, far too brief, hot pink bikini that her mother, holidaying over in Cannes, had sent her, and though Lenore was so young and so flat she could have worn only boys' trunks, Sophie felt that Garrick Saxby would not approve of Lenore's deep bra top.

Also . . . leaving Lenore's bikini . . . the girls came racing to the bus in all kinds of get-up. Towels over their shoulders like capes, or towels made into slinky skirts, into turbans, into Chinese pigtails. Certainly never neatly rolled around their bathing togs.

"Swimming girls," she called, "those of you who have beach bags, bring them with your suits and towels placed inside, those who haven't, wrap your swimmers in your towel."

"Can't we wear our togs? We always do."

They did, but G.S. might not approve. "You could catch cold," Sophie said weakly. "Anyway, even if you wear them, parcel up your towels."

"I was going to be a sheik with mine," complained Miranda.

"Well, you won't be.—Jane, I saw you flick that piece of toast at Alice."

At last the first and important meal of the day was over, and Sophie was rounding up her class, begging them to hurry, telling them not to forget their caps, not to fight for window seats (they always did) and not to forget they were young ladies. She almost implored that last as she marched them down to the small school bus that Mr. Jenkins had reversed out ready for Sophie to drive to the beach. Seeing Mr. Saxby approaching, Sophie went to get into the bus as well. One of the girls would gladly sit beside him, it was always a popular seat.

But before Sophie could climb in, too, the new headmaster had reached the mini-bus.

"Who drives?" he asked Sophie.

"I do, but I thought with you here . . ."

"You'll drive as usual," he said, and climbed into the passenger's seat.

After a moment's hesitation, Sophie obeyed.

As always, before she actually moved down the school avenue, she looked back to the school . . . to Father. Never had he not been there to wave her off. It had started the first time she had been entrusted with a vehicle after she had passed her driving test. Father had come out and warned her of the mountain curves, said : "Be careful." Ever since then his lips had framed the message. They framed the words now. Sophie started a fond little laugh that surprised her by becoming instead a hard little sob. Confused, she turned it into a cough, hoping the man now beside her in the passenger's seat did not notice.

He did. "A cold, Miss Arthur?"

"A slight one." She wondered what he would have said if she had answered:

"No, a finger on my heart just then as I looked across at Father."

She went carefully down the drive. The moment she came out of the gates on to the mountain she felt her vague unhappiness leaving her, as everything unhappy or uncomfortable or dismaying always did whenever she started the enchanted drive to the coast, that breathtaking way under the ancient zamia palms, under the huge old fig trees. It was a wonderful descent. Falls and cascades met you at every steep turn, whipbirds and wood pigeons accompanied you with their silver crack and their golden coo, lyre birds and bush turkeys meandered across the track in front of you, parrots jewelled the trees and shrubs, wallabies bounded over and koalas sometimes crossed. Clearings afforded stunning views of a flag blue sea, and, nearer, offered the pleasant sight of acres of deep green avocado and rosy red rhubarb, since in this south-east corner most of the avocado of Queensland was raised, and all the rhubarb pies of Queensland began.

The curves were sharp and steep, but they were also familiar. So familiar that ordinarily Sophie did not always keep to her own side of the road, since the traffic from the college was comfortably sparse, and any wrong side encroachment happily safe, but today she meticulously took every bend and swerve. She intended to give him nothing to complain about. It was annoying then that Laurel piped up:

"Why aren't you straightening out the road as you always do, Miss Arthur?" (That was what Sophie called it. Straightening out the road.)

She searched for a discreet reply, but found none. It

34

did not help that, by her side, the passenger chuckled.

No one else laughed, though, they had been too well briefed for laughter. Instead of bursts of song, giggles, arguments, they sat like statues.

"Dull lot, aren't they?" Garrick Saxby commented.

But as they passed the Barker Prep School for Boys at the foot of Apa, the students all turned into canines, and raised loud derisive barks, something they always did, that their seniors had done before them, that the up and coming juniors probably would, too. A bark for Barker. Sophie had forgotten about instructions for that, and she groaned.

She did not glance at Garrick Saxby, though, she turned as though nothing had happened into the Gold Coast Highway and began threading her way through the heavy holiday resort traffic to the particular beach she always took the class for their supposed instruction. High-rise apartments rose on either side, they were the tall poppies that punctuated the aspect from Apa Mountain, and seen at close quarters they were uniformly palatial, palm-festooned and quite attractive.

She passed through Labrador, Southport, Surfers' Paradise and Broadbeach down to the corner of Mermaid that she had found most applicable for her purpose. The moment she pulled up, the door of the minibus flew open and its contents spilled out and raced down to the wide, cream-tipped crescent. After all, thought Sophie, could you blame them? Children and sandy coves were synonymous, they had to merge. But undoubtedly, she thought, too, *he* could blame them. She darted Garrick Saxby a quick look . . . to find he was actually grinning.

"So they *are* normal."

"I thought you might have gathered that when we passed Barker," Sophie ventured.

35

"A bark for Barker. Well, shall we follow?" Already he was out and coming round to help Sophie down.

She had worn her swimsuit, a one-piecer in discreet navy blue as suited a mistress with children, and well covered up by a navy towelling robe. When they reached the beach she took the robe off, feeling absurdly uncomfortable over the discard, then she called:

"One row, girls. We'll do the basic movements."

They all groaned over such a foolishness, or so they considered, but they obeyed. They went laboriously through the arm drill of the Australian crawl until Lida called feelingly: "I'm tired."

Sophie said to relax for a few moments, whereupon they did what they always did when given a respite, they lost their weariness and made a beeline for their particular favourite pursuit, which was either jelly blubber collection, shell gathering, castle building or just plain splashing each other with water. But what else could you expect from a bundle of youngsters on a beach?

"Girls, we'll now try our movements in the water," Sophie said after a suitable pause. Very noticeably no one tried.

"Girls. *GIRLS*!"

"Spare yourself and your voice, Miss Arthur," Garrick Saxby said drily by Sophie's side. After a few minutes he went on: "So much for your swimming instruction."

"I'm sorry, but it's difficult on the beach."

"It's not just difficult, it's impossible." Sophie had not expected that. "Apart from waves being totally unsuitable for a lesson, there are too many distractions." He looked around at the cream sand, the pale blue water, at all the exciting things sand and water offered. Then he said: "Can you blame them?"

Sophie heaved a sigh of relief. "I always feel like

that. In the end I decided to call it beneficial for the sea air if for nothing else."

"Fair enough," he allowed magnanimously, "but it's still not teaching them to swim. You do agree with me that they must swim?"

"Oh, yes. But how? I mean until the school pool is built where else can I take the class? For the river I would need assistance, something we don't have, and the public baths are booked up."

"I believe it can be overcome," Garrick Saxby said thoughtfully. He looked at the little girls now standing unenthusiastically by the water's edge, for there is nothing more discouraging to a non-swimmer than a booming surf, and called:

"Back to your shells and jellyfish, class, but only five minutes more. After that you're *really* going to get down to work."

"How?" asked Sophie curiously.

He did not tell her, but he did add to his list of those about to work:

"You, too, Miss Arthur."

In precisely five minutes he cupped his palms round his mouth and called for attention. Sophie always did the same, and never got it, but there was something about this man, or about his voice, or perhaps his position, for he did get results. The girls got immediately into line.

"Into the bus," he ordered.

They were not so keen about that.

"Are we going back already?" they complained.

"I hadn't finished my castle."

"We're hardly here, Headmaster."

"Quiet! We're going to a place where you *can* learn to swim. After this morning's lesson which you are now going to have I expect at least two strokes from everyone."

37

They did not answer that.

Sophie in her turn also did not comment. She, too, walked unenthusiastically to the bus, where she was waved this time to the seat where he had previously sat. Getting behind the wheel, Garrick Saxby turned the small vehicle once more into the traffic.

They did not go far. They turned into one of the man-made islands that scalloped the Gold Coast. The Isle of Capri was what was known as the social island, its houses were palatial to say the least, pools for every home, marinas with groups of luxury yachts, smooth lawns, fountains, all the trappings of luxury living. Sophie wondered what was going to happen.

Garrick Saxby pulled up at perhaps the most palatial house of all. He turned to the girls and drew their attention to a sparkling pool set behind a cluster of trees.

"This is where you will practise swimming until the school pool is ready," he said.

"Won't the people mind?" called one of them dubiously.

"No."

"Do you know the people?"

"Yes."

"You're sure it's all right?"

For reply, Garrick Saxby said sternly :

"If you're not all out of the bus and lined up for Miss Arthur's instruction in two minutes you'll be glad to get into the pool to cool off." He smacked his hands together smartly and significantly, and they all piled out.

Turning to Sophie, Saxby added : "That also applies to you."

Fuming, Sophie also piled out.

She took off her robe once more and began the girls on their basic swimming exercises again. They did

38

them in the usual desultory manner; pre-swimming preparation was certainly not the most exciting activity, Sophie allowed.

After a few over-arm whirls and swirls, Garrick Saxby stopped the squad.

"All right, girls," he called, "into the pool."

They looked at him in alarm, they were strictly non-swimmers, and though the clear blueness of the circular pool was very attractive, with their lack of ability the attraction lay more in regarding, not sampling it.

"In!" he called, and slapped his hands together again in a warning fashion.

"Do you think—" came in Sophie dubiously.

"It's not a deep pool." He stopped her before she could get any further.

"Perhaps more out-of-water preparation first," Sophie persisted valiantly, for she could see that her girls were not at all eager.

"*In*-water," he proclaimed, and to make sure he took a decisive step forward, his arms outstretched.

That decided the girls, they all edged, or in the case of a few braver souls, jumped, in. Seeing him turn his attention now on her, Sophie went to jump in, too, but he stopped her.

"Just a moment, let them get the feel of it first."

Sophie did.

The girls found the "feel" better than they had expected. The sun had warmed up the pool, and, being still water, it was much gentler on the skin than the effervescent surf. They began splashing each other, plunging at each other, finding fun instead of danger.

"That's been the trouble," Saxby said to Sophie, "learning to swim, or not learning in this case, has become a chore."

"Swiming is always that in the initial stages,"

39

Sophie recalled of herself.

"Yet I see no reason why it should be. Oh, I agree that to swim well you must be taught properly, but what I wish to do, and wish very urgently, Miss Arthur, is to teach these children to keep themselves afloat first, teach them enough to save themselves in case of emergency. It's not the approved method, and I'm well aware of that, I know that all children are taught these days with the expectancy that they might become a crack performer, but I doubt if we have any potential crack performers here, and if we have well, any incorrect training, though personally I don't call it that, can soon be rectified."

"I think," deciphered Sophie delightedly, "you're going to teach them to dog-paddle."

"I'm going to teach them to keep afloat," he said, "and you're going to help me."

"Yes, sir," agreed Sophie with alacrity, for she herself had often thought that self-preservation came first and good form afterwards.

He went into the house . . . she concluded that he must know the people quite well. He came back very soon in trunks, a smiling woman came behind him. He dived neatly into the deep end of the pool and called the girls to line up.

It all went like magic. What had always . . . until Sophie had given up the impossible task . . . been a nightmare became a pleasure instead. The girls, told that they were pups, told that they had been flung into the water and had to make to the bank, reacted quite remarkably. They went under several times, but that, Saxby said by Sophie's side, was what he wanted, he wanted them on friendly terms with the underneath as well as the top of the water.

Next Garrick Saxby produced a stick and threw it in and told each in turn to retrieve it . . . *and no walk-*

ing on the pool floor to do so.

It was wonderful to see them produce three or four strokes, awkward puppy strokes but *strokes;* even timid Teresa did one and a half, and bolder Nora almost covered a quarter of the width of the pool for her return of the stick.

"Splendid," Garrick Saxby called, and he put everything into his praise. Sophie could see the girls really revelling in their achievement, and she had to give him good marks for that; children, she knew, do react to genuine recognition.

He did not prolong the lesson unduly, he did not allow them to become bored.

"Out!" he called presently and authoritatively. He turned to Sophie. "Do they bring changing clothes?"

"Mostly cover-up shorts and shirts, it's so warm there's no necessity for anything else."

"Good. As soon as they shake off their excess moisture, Mrs. Clayton will take them in for Coke and cake."

"That's very kind of her," said Sophie, a little surprised.

He did not comment on that. He resumed: "Then they can run around the garden while you and I grab a short, well-earned reward ourselves."

"Reward?" she queried.

"Teaching the young always calls for a reward. I don't know about you, Miss Arthur, but I'm damned hot."

"The pool?" she asked.

"No, I need something more bracing, and I am sure you do as well. Do you surf?"

"Oh, yes!" Sophie loved the surf.

"Then while they refresh themselves and Mrs. Clayton watches over them, we'll sneak some ocean, shall we?" With his last words he was halfway to the mini-bus, Sophie only a few steps behind him.

They were back on the beach in minutes, but not a sheltered corner this time, instead a stretch of shore where the boomers came in tall, green, strong and white-capped.

"I'll see you on the first," he challenged, and ran in.

Proud of herself that she had the ability to do just that, to see him on the first breaker, Sophie raced in as well. She was a strong swimmer, and was not far behind him in the first breaker that he had told her. It was always a good regular surf up here, singularly free of the currents and hazards of some beaches, as safe from sharks as meticulous beach and helicopter patrol could make it, so Sophie enjoyed herself.

She would have kept on blissfully enjoying herself had not Garrick Saxby, in the way all men must do, it seems, decided to show the female species the superiority that the male species possesses when it comes to physical prowess. He went out a little further. He did it in a quite friendly fashion, even raising his arm in salutation as he swam past, but Sophie was enraged. How dared he put her in her place, or so he obviously thought, like this? She would show him she was just as good as he was.

She struck out after him.

When she reached him, he frowned and indicated for her to go back. When she did not obey, he turned and retreated himself, as though setting her an example, Sophie thought, nettled. About to return, too, for after all she had established her point, she stubbornly turned back instead and swam out further again. It was a deliberate impertinence, and she knew he would know it, let her know he knew it, but she could not resist showing off. She grinned to herself.

Out here the sea moved in long rhythmic ripples, no whitecaps now, just smooth deep green swells. The water, as it always was in this balmy corner of Queensland, had a soft pleasant feel. Each time Sophie went on top of a long ripple the sun touched her warmly. With no waves to ride, no body surfing to perform, she simply relaxed and floated also, if she had been honest enought to admit it, gloated. That should teach Mr. Saxby all about the weaker sex!

Her first alarm came several long ripples later when she looked around and saw that she had drifted out more that the extra few yards she had intended. The shore looked quite a long way off.

The second alarm came with Garrick Saxby's alerting voice. At once, like all surfers, she thought of sharks. There was an excellent shark record up here, the shore and helicopter patrols saw to that; also for some reason the shark seemed to favour cooler waters, for he was not, and never had been, as prevalent as further south. A long swell bore her up and a quick glance to the beach assured her that the safety flags were still up and waving briskly, so she was quite all right. What, then? she thought, irritated. Did that man think she was incapable of looking after herself?

Then suddenly she was realizing that that was just what she could not do. She could not look after herself. All at once there was simply too much water, too much very deep, very green, vast, endless water. It was beneath her, over her, around her, far too much of it. Every time a ripple went past to build up into a wave to race into the beach she was buried and suffocated with it. When she came up for breath, it seemed no time before another big boomer in the making was burying her all over again.

She had no thoughts of going out further now, she only wanted to get in. At once, realizing she was tiring, she began to tread water. Floating would have afforded better rest, but if she floated it could well be outward, for she had no idea of the trend of the tide.

She soon knew, though. Changing her water treading to a few arm strokes to edge her further shoreward, she saw she was making no progress at all. She tried swimming a little harder and quicker, and succeeded at first, but only for a few moments while her burst of energy helped her. After that she went quickly out again.

Garrick's next shout came at the same time as a much deeper and far more thrusting ripple of water. This often happened, Sophie knew. The surf could roll in rhythmically for hours, then suddenly, and for no apparent reason, build up to a very large wave . . . to a series of large waves. That was what was happening now. There was a sudden build-up beginning to send a procession of large boomers on to the beach, and the acceleration was being enacted right here over her, underneath her, all round her. Sophie felt water everywhere. She swallowed some, and that was her undoing. She coughed and swallowed more. She looked around and seemed enclosed in steep walls of water.

"Help me!" she tried to call, but she knew it would only be a croak.

It couldn't have been only that, though, for Garrick Saxby's voice answered her at once.

"You don't need help," he called quite coolly and casually, "just turn on your back and take a spell. Then we'll hit for shore together." He was near her, only some yards away. He was coming comfortingly nearer.

"I can't." Now all thought of female superiority, or even female equality, was gone. Sophie was plainly and simply frightened.

"Of course you can," he told her, still casually. "If you want to, you can hold on to me."

44

"I——"

"Do just that, Sophie. Put your hand on my shoulder. Rest. Relax. Then we'll set off."

"I——"

"Don't talk, there's a good girl."

He was so calm, so assured and so assuring, so—so gentle, Sophie felt strength ebbing back to her. She did as he said, put her hands on his shoulders, and the big, strong muscular masculinity of them seemed to strengthen her even more.

"Care to try it now?" Still the calm, assuring, gentle voice, and Sophie mumbled "Yes", and, stroke by stroke beside him, she set off.

All the way he kept up the gentle reassurance, the cheerful 'there's nothing to it', and Sophie reacted completely. Then at last he said: "You can put your feet down now and walk" . . . and at the same time he put out his hand and pushed her under, right under, and held her there a long punishing moment. Then he let her splutter up.

"Why did you do that?" she gasped when she could find words.

"Hair of the dog," he answered coolly. "I didn't want you to come out of this with a dread of the sea."

"I don't believe you," she said angrily, "you were punishing me."

"What if I was? I've never seen such a rotten display in all my life. It was all right trying to prove you were as good as the next one, but did you have to stage a near-disaster to do it? Oh, yes, you did, my girl. You were out of control out there, you were bested. Had I not been around you would have been written off as lost at sea, probably eaten by some hungry maneater by now."

"And no loss, *you* would have thought," she flung.

"Certainly little loss—anyway, you young fool, do

45

you always have to make your point so factually?"

"I'm sorry," Sophie said, "I was reckless and inconsiderate, but did you have to bring it home to me in that way? By half-drowning me? That was no hair of the dog."

"No," he agreed, "there was a certain amount of venom in it as well. That sea was pretty high, and I could have lost my own life saving yours. Incidentally, you haven't thanked me."

"Thank you," said Sophie.

They walked to the beach, silently took up their wraps, then they went up to the parked mini and back to the Isle of Capri house where the children had been left with Mrs. Clayton. Sophie thanked the lady for having them, then they all climbed into the bus, Garrick Saxby nodding Sophie to the seat beside the driver once more, and they started back up the foothills to their hinterland beyond.

It was a silent journey for quite some time for Sophie, but the girls had lost their imposed restraint and were chattering excitedly. They were all very pleased with themselves and what they had achieved.

"It's rather like a fisherman showing you the length of his catch," grinned Garrick Saxby, evidently deciding to drop the surf incident. "Those few strokes are increasing every minute. By the way they're stretching the distance you won't need to take them down there any more."

"Was that the plan? To make it a regular thing?"

"Well, you didn't think I intended finishing it at that." He negotiated a bend.

"No, but I was thinking that Mrs. Clayton might not be so keen."

"Why shouldn't she? It's all in a day's work."

"A day's work, but——"

"She is my housekeeper," said Garrick Saxby, and

he started up the first foothill from the coastal flats.

"You mean that the——"

"That the house is mine? Yes. Good lord, you didn't think I'd intrude like that on a friend?"

"I really don't know what you would do," said Sophie. "After all, I barely know you."

"That will be rectified," he promised. "Living as close under one roof, how couldn't it be?"

"Then you won't be commuting up from the coast to the school?"

"Not, anyway, while I'm less than a family man," he replied.

"You intend to become one?"

"I do." For a moment he took his eyes off the road and looked fully at Sophie. The look challenged her, but she interpreted it as a rebuke for her curiosity. All the same she found she still had to comment.

"Usually headmasters are resident," she heard herself insinuating.

"It depends on the headmaster's wife, on Mrs. Headmaster." Again he looked at her. "As Miss Headmistress yourself at one time, and with an eye to something else, what would you choose if you were in the position?"

"I was never Miss Headmistress."

"And never had an eye on being Miss Headmaster?"

"If by that you mean didn't I see myself as the headmaster's daughter, yes, I expect I did."

"Then what would Miss Headmaster choose?"

"Miss and Mrs. are vastly different," snapped Sophie.

"In their preferences as well?"

"All this doesn't refer to me and it never will. Can we change the subject, please?"

He shrugged, drove for a few moments, then started

47

in completely different strain. "You know this district, Miss Arthur?"

"I came here as a child. My father was widowed and it was not every school that would accept a resident male teacher with a small daughter."

"But Honor would?"

"You knew her?"

"Yes." A pause. "Tell me about this place, what it was like then."

"Beautiful. Always beautiful. I don't think the Gold Coast was ever, or ever will be, less than beautiful."

"You don't resent what man has done to it?"

"I think if anything man has enhanced it. The mountains, of course, are still as they were, but even the rest, changed though it may be, is lovely."

"Any history?"

"You mean you don't know it?"

"No."

"It all started with a sawyer, Neddy Harper. Neddy discovered the Gold Coast and the hinterland in 1842. He was very young . . . only in his teens . . . but he had an adventurous streak and he crossed the Tweed Valley, where he lived, through dense forests to come to—well, paradise." Sophie gave a little embarrassed laugh.

"Yes?" he encouraged quite sincerely.

"Although he was so youthful, Neddy still established a wharf to cater for boats using the Nerang River. He began the first commercial enterprise, the first of many." She glanced back at the high rise buildings, those tall poppies of the flats.

"The natives called the region 'Kurrungul' because of the plentiful supply of hardwood. But there were pines and cedar, too, to lure the timbercutters, and Neddy set up cedar camps. The timber was cut up on

48

our mountains, then floated down our river, then joined in long rafts to be taken to Brisbane. More settlers came in."

"Yes?" he encouraged again.

"I suppose it all went on from there. Little Elston had to."

"Elston?" he queried.

"Surfers was called that until someone said it was a paradise, not Elston, and so it became just that." Sophie gave another little embarrassed laugh. "The first school enrolled only twenty-three children."

"A far cry from its state schools and colleges of today," Garrick Saxby said. He went on : "I know about Apa College . . . it was originally Apa homestead, I believe, and the lady of the house had to teach her three young daughters since it was too far for them to travel for their education, and the daughters brought their friends, and the friends their friends, and so a school grew."

"Then stopped growing," came in Sophie. "I just can't picture the new era. I just can't see Apa as co-ed."

"You're a Women's Libber?" he asked politely.

"No. Also I'm all for co-education. But Apa?"

"It remains to be seen," he advised. "Anyway, I trust your doubts will not encourage any non-co-operation."

"No," said Sophie.

They drove on for a while, leaving the crumpled blue-green carpet of foothills to skim round the sometimes sheer curves of the plateau. Sophie broke in on his silence once to indicate a cedar stand.

When they passed one of the several district studs, Garrick Saxby looked across at the blood horses grazing in the lush paddocks and told Sophie that riding most certainly would feature in any new curriculum.

"How are you on that?" he inquired.

"As phys ed teacher I should be able to handle it," she answered.

"But you're not, are you?" he pointed out blandly.

"A horsewoman? How would you know?"

"Not a phys ed graduate."

"No. Nor am I a nature study mistress, but I can sort out flowers," she said with spirit.

"Good for you. I like my teachers to have get-up-and-go." He nodded at her as she looked at him with disbelief at such an award. "But not too much get-up-and-go, Miss Arthur. Just don't get out of your depth again, please."

"I'll do my best."

"Said she," he came in adroitly, "wishing she could retort instead 'You do your best and sign up someone else instead.' "

"Why don't you?" she asked curiously.

"I can't at present. After we've settled and found out whom we want and don't want, it may be a different story."

"For both of us?" Sophie murmured.

"Both? But I won't be leaving. Not, anyway, for some time."

"I meant Father and myself."

"Your father won't," he answered quickly.

"If I went, Father would," Sophie told him.

"Then we must keep you, mustn't we?"

"You mean my father is needed?"

A slight pause, then: "Yes."

"Yet not as headmaster."

"You're still on that," he said in disgust.

"Why shouldn't I be? When a man has been deputy all that time—"

He slackened the pace a little to allow himself to

50

turn fully if briefly on her.

"Miss Arthur, have you asked your father if he wants to be head?"

"Yes."

"And his answer?"

"No. But that's typical of Father."

"What is?"

"Stepping back, stopping in the background, never asserting himself."

"Because he didn't need to," said the man quite unexpectedly, and his voice was warm. "Never our Mr. Headmistress."

Sophie knew she should have felt proud because of that warm praise, but somehow she couldn't . . . or wouldn't. Mr. Headmistress who never became Headmaster, she thought.

He halted the argument by commenting on the bellbirds clamouring their song above the noise of the engine, on the tympanic surge of the many streams racing down the gorges, on the emerald necklet made up by the myriad trees running up the mountain's shoulder and extending across the ridge, but Sophie, although she loved it all, barely responded now, and presently he gave up.

Even the children had stopped their chatter . . . tired, probably . . . but the silence grew, and grew, until it could almost be *felt*.

Sophie, anyway, felt it, and she sensed something suddenly tightening around her, growing tighter still with every yard nearer to the school. Once she even put her hand up to her throat.

"What is it?" he broke his silence to ask in quick concern.

"Nothing. Nothing. I'm being silly—all at once I felt—"

"Yes?"

"Nothing. Why are you stopping, Mr. Saxby?"

"From the lack of noise at the back it seems our swimmers have flaked out. Well, they're not getting away with that, they can walk the rest of the way back over the ridge."

"It's easily half a mile."

"It won't kill them, in fact it will do them good."

"Shall I go, too?"

"Good grief, no, you don't have to wet nurse them all the time, they can find their own way, surely?"

"Yes, but—"

"Out, girls. A walk back will give you exercise." He had turned to his busload to issue the order, and Sophie turned, too. To her surprise the girls were obeying him with a minimum of complaints.

He started off again. Now he drove quickly, Sophie noted, he seemed to be looking directly ahead of them, not around as before. Looking only to the school.

Sophie looked, too.

"There's some activity," she said, narrowing her eyes up the hill. "Staff seem to be going here and there. Has something happened, do you think? I can't see Father."

I can't see Father. It was not until they reached the big gates that those four words came rushing back to Sophie. Rushing with a sickening significance. She remembered her odd feeling as they had left today, recalled it hollowly. "I can't see Father." She said it again . . . said it to the man.

"Mr. Saxby, I can't see Father. Everyone seems to be running around, and something seems to have happened, but . . . but I can't see Father."

"No, little one." Garrick Saxby said it so quietly, so gently for a big, hard, self-contained man, that Sophie looked at him in question. She did not actually ques-

52

tion him, though. She just sat very still as he ran the
bus up the drive and stopped at the big doors of the
school. Then he came round to Sophie's side and lifted
her out.

CHAPTER THREE

So much for fingers on your heart, for presciences, premonitions, what-have-yous, Sophie was half crying, half laughing a few minutes later. For Father was sitting by the window in Honor's apartment taking in the panoramic view at the same time as he took it easy. The dear fraud, Sophie thought, as she fairly leapt on him to hug him.

"What's all this about?" Mr. Arthur objected mildly. "A man sits down for a piece of quiet and an avalanche descends on him!"

"All forty-odd kilograms of it," came in Garrick Saxby, who had come behind Sophie up the stairs to the front suite. "I must tell you, sir, you raised a less than calm daughter."

"There appeared to be a lot of coming and going," Sophie defended herself, rather foolish now that her unnamed fear was over, "and you weren't in it." She could have added that Garrick Saxby, too, had behaved in rather an unusual manner: he had driven very fast up the hill, he had agreed "No, little one" when she had pointed out the fact of Father's absence. Agreed gently.—*Gently*?

"You're a pair of panic merchants," complained Mr. Arthur, "as are your staff too, Garrick. An old man clumsily walks into the newel post and all the college is in chaos. That pulsating crowd you saw from down the hill was the school first aid team trying themselves out on my injured knee."

"Was it injured, sir?" asked Saxby quickly.

"Or perhaps the calf muscle. I don't know until Jasper comes." Mr. Arthur was looking very steadily at the headmaster, had Sophie noticed.

But Sophie didn't.

"Oh, Father," she came in anxiously, "how did it happen? Did you feel faint? Did you have a black-out? Did—"

"I simply forgot to put on my glasses," deflated Mr. Arthur, "and consequently walked into the post. I've probably marked it. Sorry, Garrick."

"On behalf of the post, forget it, sir. On behalf of the school, please do whatever Doctor Jasper tells you when he comes, we don't want to pay out compensation on cartilages."

"I can't see anything wrong with the cartilage," muttered Sophie, examining the knee. She thought that the headmaster could have left out that compensation bit.

"Cartilages don't pop out like carbuncles; also you have the wrong leg," Garrick Saxby said drily. "Ah, here's Jasper now." He crossed over to Sophie and actually began impelling her to the door.

"I'll stop and help," she began . . . but by the time Doctor Jasper, the school and mountain doctor, was in the room, Sophie and Garrick were out of it.

"Really, this is quite ridiculous!" Sophie fumed, not caring about her forcible exclusion.

"I agree. You would embarrass both your father and the doctor fiddling around in there."

"I wouldn't fiddle."

"Well, you wouldn't do anything constructive, you're not a nurse."

"Nor a phys ed teacher, nor a nature study mistress. You could say I'm nothing at all."

"I could. However, you've said it for me."

Angrily, Sophie reminded him: "You said something rather odd yourself. When I became alarmed and pointed out that Father was not to be seen among the milling crowd—"

"Crowd?"

"Well, rather more than the usual gathering, it was then you said" . . . she hesitated . . . "you said 'Yes, little one.' "

"Well?" he asked coolly.

"Why?" she asked back.

"Because he wasn't to be seen, of course."

"And—the other?"

"Little one? You're not large."

"But—but said like that?"

"Like what?"

"Like—kindly," she explained.

"I'm not unkind."

"Sympathetically, I mean." A pause. "Gently."

"You have imagination, Miss Arthur," he remarked, and it successfully douched Sophie.

"How long is that doctor going to be?" she chaffed presently.

"As long as it takes him to bandage up your father."

"But he doesn't require bandaging."

"*Nurse* Arthur speaking?"

"Well, the joint looked and felt all right."

"We'll see," Garrick Saxby said with finality, and he turned as the door opened and the doctor came out again.

"Patient as comfortable as can be expected," Doctor Jasper reported with fatuous cheerfulness. "Rest, rest, then more rest until the injury knits."

"What injury?" asked Sophie.

"Oh, hullo. Sophie." Doctor Jasper smiled at her. "Unfortunate that the newel post bumped into your father."

"You're being so heavily funny, Doctor Jasper, it isn't funny," Sophie informed him. She had known the doctor since she had been a small girl. "Is it his knee, or his calf, or his ankle, or his—"

For a moment, so ephemeral a moment it was barely even that, the doctor paused.

"Pulled," he said triumphantly at last, "quite definitely pulled. Bandaging and rest will fix it."

"But—"

"I hear you start your male intake tomorrow, Saxby. Well, all the better for trade, and I include our medical variety. When it comes to common . . . but rewarding . . . everyday accidents, give me boys any time. But at other times" . . . a fond smile at Sophie . . . "a pretty girl will do." He tweaked Sophie's straight, candy-coloured hair, and left them.

"Silly old fool!" fumed Sophie. Without waiting for Garrick Saxby's permission, which she wouldn't have taken, anyway, she turned and went quickly into the room.

And there sat Father, leg propped on a stool, and bandaged from ankle to thigh.

"So they've trussed you up, sir," Saxby, by Sophie's side, said wryly. There was more than a hint of laughter in the wryness.

"It's not funny." Sophie turned furiously on him.

"I agree," said Mr. Arthur plaintively. "How would you like to be put on a shelf like this?"

"How would you like to be one teacher short at a very crucial time?" came back Saxby. "We take in our first parcel of boys tomorrow and need every hand on deck."

"I'll do what I can from my chair," promised Mr. Arthur, "and I assure you a double effort on both our behalfs from my daughter Sophie."

57

Sophie had to put on a gracious face and tell the head she would do just that.

"Thank you," Garrick Saxby said in a rather unconvinced voice.

"Are you to be X-rayed, Father?" Sophie asked.

"No, the damage was apparent to Jasper. All I need is to rest the—well, whatever has to be rested."

"Yes. Whatever." Now Sophie was even less convinced. But there was no chance to probe any more, the talk left Mr. Arthur and his inopportune contact with the newel post and centred on tomorrow's influx. The junior grade would arrive first. It was agreed that Father could do the enrolment if Mr. Saxby could get him downstairs into the office, and with the gardener, the janitor and the headmaster that should be no worry. In fact everything seemed to be fitting into place. Sophie remarked so a little pointedly, and had the satisfaction of two distinctly alerted glances at her.

But nothing was said.

"I'll tell you what particulars I want recorded," the headmaster told Mr. Arthur, and Sophie excused herself, and went out.

The first person she met was Marion Javes, who called sympathetically down the corridor :

"How's Mr. Headmistress? Oh, dear me, how silly, but that name *sticks*. How is he, Sophie? We all got such a shock when we found him on the floor. At once the school first aid team got into its stride. Apart from Angela fainting when she saw Mr. Headmistress . . . Mr. Arthur . . . and Jean poking Brenda in the stomach with the end of the stretcher, it went off very well, I think."

"Doctor Jasper says it's pulled," said Sophie vaguely, but then she *was* vague. What was pulled? She waited for Marion to ask, but Marion only tut-tutted and said how much worse it could be.

"Things can always be worse," she declared wisely.

"Like the senior boys after we've finished with the juniors," Sophie suggested.

"My dear, we just don't know, do we, some small boys are angels and some big boys are demons and vice versa. Time alone will tell." Marion busied herself off.

Sophie found the rest of the staff and questioned them discreetly about Father's accident, but no one knew anything, they had come down the passage and found him on the floor. No, not knocked out, and not in any pain. Just one of those things, poor Mr. Headmistress. Oh, dear, they giggled, we'll have to stop saying that now we have a headmaster. The talk left Father and went eagerly, excitedly to what tomorrow would bring, and, more enjoyable still, to the ones to help bring it. Three male teachers, to be precise. Three more the day after, with the arrival of the senior school. It was all very stimulating, ran the chatter . . . male conversation would be a refreshing change . . . like a need for co-ed there was a need for different sex outlooks in teachers. After all, male and female created He them.

Sophie escaped.

It wasn't that she was a Women's Libber, it was just that the happy acceptance all round irritated her, she told herself, making her way to the gym. When she first had had the role of phys ed mistress bestowed on her, she had made the gymnasium a regular call every day so as to keep herself at least one step ahead of her younger so presumably more agile girls. Then during one session she had discovered that work on the horse, or the swing, or bar, or simply dancing had released something in her, relaxed her so completely that any frustrations she thought she felt became simply that: thinking. So she set to work now, not bothering to

59

change into a covering track suit, to do push-ups, back flips, bicycles in the air.

"No." The voice came from the door of the gym, a male voice, and at once, since he was the only male apart from Father (unless you counted Mr. Jenkins and George who wouldn't come to the gym, anyway), Sophie thought of the headmaster. But the voice had been more boyish, much more amiable. Sophie came down from the suspended position into which she had heaved herself and looked across the hall to a smiling young man.

"Name of Bill Bethel." The man came forward, loose, lean, whipcord almost, clear blue eyes in a clear tan skin. He just had to be Sports, Sophie thought.

"Sophie Arthur, phys ed," she introduced herself. "If you were saying I was doing it wrongly, you could be right—I've never been trained."

"You were doing it magnificently," Bill Bethel awarded, "but making it hard for yourself."

"I wanted to, I had some spleen to work out."

"Good for you . . . or should I say bad for the spleen? But your kids might find it easier doing it this way." Although he was dressed in creased flannels and white shirt, he got down on the floor.

"Oh, no," Sophie protested, "at least use a mat."

"It all comes out in the wash. That's the first thing a gymnast learns—always buy things that launder. How is it that gyms get so dusty, do you think, not enough ground exercises for the brats to get rid of the grime for you?" He was laughing as he shook himself.

"You haven't shown me where I went wrong," said Sophie. "No, please don't. I mean not now. I mean wait till you're undressed. I mean . . . oh, dear!" They both laughed.

When they had finished laughing, Bill Bethel said: "Well, that's a good beginning. I was rather dreading teaming up with a Morris Dance devotee."

"Why do men always trot out poor Morris? Actually it's a man's dance, not a woman's."

"And can be very vigorous, too," he agreed. "Perhaps I should have said eurythmics."

Sophie tilted her chin. "We can do anything boys do."

"Football?"

"We—ll—"

"I'm only teasing you, of course." He smiled. He had a very nice smile. He looked around. "It seems a fairly ample gym."

"All the school is ample, otherwise we wouldn't be absorbing you."

"You know what? We were given the impression we were absorbing you.'

"Then," suggested Sophie, liking Bill Bethel more every minute, "let's meet halfway."

"I'll second that." He put a firm hand in Sophie's.

They talked easily together until Sophie saw to her surprise that dusk was creeping in. Bill Bethel was surprised, too. "I'll have to get back to the coast," he said.

"To Kingsley College?"

"Academy," he grinned. "I only raced up to have a preview of my future battleground. Now I must hurry back. Tonight's our last night."

"Is that sad?"

"I don't believe so, I think this co-ed move is a good one. The mountains in place of the coast is good, too. Everything is good." He looked steadily at Sophie.

"Male and female . . ." she heard herself begin. She blushed and broke off.

He smiled at her, no wry amusement as when the headmaster smiled, just genuine niceness. "I second that."

61

"You'd better go," she reminded him a little shyly, "the curves are quite treacherous if you don't know them. Especially at dusk. Besides, tomorrow is a big day."

"I can see that now," he said seriously, and again he looked at Sophie.

She went to the drive with him where his small roadster waited.

"I never said goodbye to the headmaster," he remembered. "Will you tell him, Miss Arthur?"

"Yes, Mr. Bethel."

"Tomorrow, then."

"Tomorrow." She watched him start down the drive.

She went back through the garden and was ashamed at the lightness and the stimulation in her . . . just like those others, she thought distastefully.

As she bent instinctively to pull out a weed she noticed a man's trouser leg in the next bed. Glancing up, she saw that the trouser leg belonged to Garrick Saxby. He was looking around him and being very much the lord of the manor, she thought.

"You appear very satisfied with your territory," she said, piqued at his presence in what had become her corner, ostensibly making it sound playful (she hoped) but meaning it less playfully.

"Not quite satisfied, but headed in that direction. And do you know how you look, Miss Arthur? Like a kitten who has just tasted cream." A pause. "Young Bethel inspected the gym, didn't he?"

"If you know he did why are you asking me?"

"He said he was going over, but lots of the younger breed say things they don't carry out."

"That sounds almost like a warning," Sophie interpreted.

"Do not trust him, gentle maiden, you mean? It

was not intended like that."

"Nor required, Mr. Saxby, if you were issuing a discreet insinuation. Incidentally, Mr. Bethel gave me a message for you."

"Yes?"

"Goodbye," Sophie said baldly.

"Was that all?"

"Yes. He'd forgotten to say it to you himself."

"So asked you?"

"I just told you."

The dinner bell clanged. Good gracious, Sophie thought, she hadn't washed yet.

"You're on duty, too," he said hatefully, apparently reading her dismay. "Just a lick will have to do, won't it, but I would get rid of that dust."

"Am I dusty?"

"Across your back and seat."

She flushed. "I was on the floor. So was Mr. Bethel. It's amazing how gymnasiums get dusty. More ground exercises needed to sweep it away, we both agreed."

"You're in agreement already? That's fine. Just what a co-ed establishment needs. Now please get to your table or there'll be *dis*agreement."

"What about Father?" she asked.

"He's having his dinner sent up. Will you please hurry, Miss Arthur. You're to superintend the Fifth, I think. Also, next time that you do floor exercises, kindly leave yourself enough margin to wash properly as well as dust."

"Yes, sir."

"Saxby is sufficient."

"Yes, Saxby." She did not know why she said it, it was an awful impertinence and she would never have done it had she thought first.

She became aware that he was looking at her. No, *through* her . . . and, really, she couldn't blame him.

"Yes, Mr. Saxby," she said hastily. "Yes, Head master."

She hurried off.

"What will we eat when they come?" mused Bettina at tea.

"Take your elbows off the table, Bettina, and we'l eat what we're eating now."

"Yuk," said Julia.

Sophie ignored that, but she did not ignore Wendy's plaintive:

"Will we have to wait on them? Shall we have to wear little aprons and caps?"

"Certainly not. Just because they're boys they're not waited on."

"My mother says all men are waited on."

"Perhaps your mother has spoiled your brothers."

"There's none. That's why she only had me. Because men have to be waited on."

"It's not always like that, Wendy. Belinda, eat your sweet."

"Rice?" grumbled Belinda.

"Do boys eat rice?"

"Lucky pigs if they don't."

On and on it went, always coming back to boys. Sophie sighed with relief when the meal finished, but she knew the staff room would be worse still. Men, men, men. And yet Bill Bethel had seemed a very pleasant type. Helpful, too. She must get a few hints from him.

She went upstairs to Honor's suite and found her father at the window. He looked very comfortable, obviously the leg wasn't bothering him at all, and Sophie got a chair and sat beside him. They watched the moon rise out of the distant Pacific, a wine-dark sea now, because the scarlet of the setting sun had left some of its red behind it. In a few hours the red would be navy blue. The penthouses of the tall-rise buildings with their punctuated lights already were gathering crowns of stars.

"Oh, it's beautiful, Father."

"Yes, Sophie, and that's another reason why I should be here. I mean—"

"Darling, you sound as though there was a shortage of time," Sophie giggled lovingly.

"What kind of day was it?" asked Mr. Arthur a little hurriedly, though Sophie did not notice.

"*You* should have that answer," she laughed.

"I mean apart from a clumsy parent, Sophie."

"Not bad, not bad at all." Sophie decided not to tell him about the surfing incident.

A warm, soft, embracing silence grew between them.

"Mustn't linger too long," said Mr. Arthur, "big day tomorrow."

"Will it be too much for you, darling?" Sophie fussed.

"Sitting back while the rest of you run around!"

"Do you think it will be a good thing, Father?"

"Male and female?"

"Created He them," finished Sophie a little impatiently. "Everyone is saying that."

"So?" Father asked.

"Well, Honor never brought it in."

"But she had that idea in mind. Yes" . . . as Sophie looked surprised . . . "she did. That's why Garrick Saxby—"

"Oh, yes, he mentioned Honor."

"Of course he would mention her, he—"

There was sudden pandemonium from the direction of the Third Grade's dormitory, and since the Third, although she took all classes, was Sophie's personal allotment, she hurried along at once.

"I bagged it first," one of her angels was claiming fiercely.

"I have a cousin coming, so it should be me."

"I thought of it!"

"What is all this?" demanded Sophie. "And who brought this in?"

She did not shudder at the large lizard, though, you did not live up on Apa without becoming used to a reptile or so. Never snakes, but certainly harmless blues, frillies, an occasional goanna, they caused no dismay, indeed several of the girls enticed them for pets.

"Alison is going to put Luke into one of the boys' beds when they come."

"Luke is this fellow, I presume?"

"Yes, and it's not fair."

"It certainly isn't fair for Luke, he doesn't deserve squashing, which could easily happen. Besides, the boys could reciprocate."

They looked at her, and Sophie said: "Could pay you back. Remember, they've been on the coast and could have a crab or so in a bottle waiting for just such an occasion. Now" . . . to a rather chastened group . . . "lights out in five minutes."

When she went back to her father, Sophie sighed: "The older ones are anticipating the change and the younger ones are anticipating the change . . . but for vastly different reasons."

"It's remarkable how a few years alters an outlook. However, they all shake down in the end."

They sat in comfortable silence until it was time for bed.

The one-time overseer's, or property manager's, house, the old homestead's barns and stables had been done over to cater for the new staff and new school until more modern accommodation could be built. As the residents were to be entirely male it made everything much easier. Bare stained floors with thrown-down rugs were quicker than carpeting, and uncluttered brown furniture easier than dressing tables with the frilled skirts that young females inevitably expect. Sophie, shown over Kingsley . . . the sign on the coast school gate had already been transferred up to Apa and made into a "house" insignia for the new quarters . . . was quite impressed. Considering the very short time he had had, Garrick Saxby had achieved results.

There were to be no lessons today. All the girls, from senior down to junior down to pre-elementary, were asked instead to spend the time making the newcomers welcome. The seniors naturally were not over-keen to exert themselves for a bunch of small boys, as today's influx promised, but the contemporaries of the small boys frankly were looking forward to it . . . but for different reasons than the adults hoped. There was a light of battle in their young eyes. Sophie hoped that Father had been right when he had said: ". . . they all shake down."

Promptly at ten, the first bus panted up the hinterland road. One moment the quadrangle was empty save for its surrounding square of girls, then the next moment it was full of junior boys.

All sorts of boys, all sizes from midgets of six to promising giants of eleven. Dark boys, fair boys, several reds, a number of tows and sandies. Billy Bunter boys who . . . like Andrea . . . would have to be watched at meals (and between meals). The inevitable monkeys who were here, there and everywhere, but most often, it seemed, at the hurting end of a tantalising pony tail. Sophie at once had four reports of hair pulled out by the roots, which was discounted, and one of the end of a coiffure being dipped in paint, which she did not discount, since Ella's fair pageboy had a distinct flip-up of bright orange.

"Has one of your dev—pupils a can of orange paint?" she asked a master, following it with a pleased: "Oh, it's Mr. Bethel!"

"Miss Arthur," the sports master beamed. "Yes. It will be Anderson. He seems always to come prepared."

"He'll find some preparation here," Sophie warned.

"Good. It's what he needs."

Bill Bethel looked around at the milling crowd, small people but still milling. "Poor Headmaster," he sympathized.

Garrick Saxby was not to be seen, so Sophie said feelingly that she thought the "poor" should be for the teachers. It wasn't easy settling in newcomers.

"Ah, but he's dealing with Parents. Don't you know about Parents? They're conducted strictly to the front of the house and no doubt now are taking tea with Mr. Saxby, though I'd say he isn't taking tea with them."

"Why not?" asked Sophie. She felt angered that she had not been asked to take tea, too; looking around she could see at least four of the women teachers conspicuously absent.

"Too busy," grinned Bill Bethel. "You know how it is with new boys."

"I don't."

"New girls, then. They're not that, not boys and not girls. They're delicate souls. They're gossamer. They're anything but flesh and blood and snub noses and freckles. Mr. Saxby will hear that seventeen times instead of drinking tea. When he does get round to it, the tea will be cold."

"Why seventeen?"

Another grin from Bill Bethel. "Because that's the

68

new intake. We have exactly seventeen freshers."

"But Mr. Saxby would know all this before, he was head of Kingsley prior to this move."

"Oh, no, he was Head nowhere."

"Oh, wasn't he then!" Sophie found pleasure in that.

"Only Head of the Heads," deflated Bill Bethel, "he was director of all these schools, the top of the top. You could say the cream of the cream."

"Yet never headmaster," Sophie repeated. She looked across to the Head's office and tried to hide a grin of satisfaction. I hope they're killing him, she was thinking, for living as near as she had to Honor, she knew just how ragged a Head can get by the end of a first day. And . . . almost hugging herself . . . there was another first day tomorrow. Serves him right for ousting Father.

"Why is he Head here, then?" she asked Bill Bethel. "A demotion or what?"

Bill looked at her quickly, then glanced away.

"It would only be pending," he said.

"You mean temporary till a permanent Head is decided?"

"Yes." Bill must have decided that work called, for he excused himself and hurried away.

Sophie bustled around in the customary manner, though it wasn't customary really, this time it was boys, not girls, and instead of a matron to whom to offer her assistance there appeared to be a kind of major-domo. Sophie privately thought that was going too far, small boys were essentially just small boys, but the Nabob, as the plump, pleasant house director told her he was called, looked so sympathetic as well as efficient that she found herself accepting him. Not that she had any alternative, she thought with a smile.

When a message came from the Headmaster

(whether pending, temporary or what-have-you, still, at this present moment, the Headmaster) directing her assistance in the office, she told the Nabob, and he nodded for her to go. So Mr. Saxby was finding the going tough, deduced Sophie of the message. Too bad, she thought insincerely, like all strictly book men, which Bill Bethel had just indicated he was, apparently the practical side of a business was not so easy as it seemed on paper.

Deliberately she took her time in obeying. The Nabob naturally needed a lot of help, for Apa was new to him, he had to learn the layout of the dormitories, the ablution block, servery, all the offices.

When she finished assisting him, the boys looked ready for sustenance, so she helped deal out cookies and milk. After that she rounded up some female miscreants, bent on starting the first battle of the sexes, junior variety.

Finally . . . looking down at herself . . . she felt she had to change to serve in no less exalted a post than the head office.

It had been a gooey business, she thought, back in Honor's suite, small boys were always sticky from sweets or sweat, she would really have to shower before she presented herself at the door marked Headmaster.

In all it was an hour before Sophie walked down the corridor and knocked on the portal with the gold lettering. Her knock was not answered at once, but it was not the murmur of anxious parents drowning the discreet rat-tat that did that, for Sophie, listening closely, could hear no parents.

She knocked again, tellling herself that inside the office was so quiet she could have heard a clock tick. As a matter of fact a clock chimed, and, counting the strokes, Sophie was astounded to find out how late it

70

was, how long she had taken.

The door was opening. Behind the figure opening it there was nobody . . . nobody at all.

"I was held up," Sophie said. She did not feel so pleased with herself now.

"By your neck, I trust." Garrick Saxby stepped back to let her pass by him into the room.

"The next time I send for you, Miss Arthur," he said, "come. The next time I direct you, obey."

He nodded to a chair.

CHAPTER FOUR

Garrick Saxby had sat on that executive side of the desk the last time she had been in this office, Sophie thought wryly, and she had resented it, believed he had seated himself incorrectly. Now she knew he had taken up his rightful position on that occasion . . . but she still resented it. All the more since he was *not*, so Bill Bethel had said, a Headmaster. He might be the top brass, cream of the cream, *but he was not strictly a Headmaster*.

She kept repeating this silently to herself to lend her courage, for the look on the "Headmaster's" face was anything but cordial. She trusted he had not worn a face like that for the new boys, otherwise the cots in the dormitories would be unslept in tomorrow, an alert put out for scared-off, homebound juniors. The parents, too, would not have been happy relinquishing their treasures to the owner of that severe countenance.

However, he could not have been quite the way he appeared now, for he put his hands up to his face and began manipulating the muscles.

"I've smiled so much even the cheekbones are weary," he sighed.

"The penalty of being pleasant, Headmaster," Sophie said blithely; now that she knew he was not a Headmaster, not *really*, it made it easier to be amiable.

He looked at her narrowly, her blitheness immediately suspect; she had gulped quite visibly before

72

whenever she gave him this title, but now she was fairly trilling it out.

"On the subject of penalties," he said drily, "you are on the receiving side, Miss Arthur."

"Because I'm late. I was bowed down with work." She made the excuse triumphantly.

"Yes" . . . drily . . . "I saw you through the window."

"The Nabob . . . I mean the boys' house director required assistance. After that I had to help with refreshments."

"You also had a message to attend here. When I send a message like that I mean At Once, Miss Arthur."

"You didn't say so on the note."

"I naturally took it that you would obey orders like orders should be obeyed. On the double."

She looked at him pityingly. "Girls don't do that. Not martial stuff, I mean. Guides, perhaps, when told by their patrol leader, but not—" She stopped abruptly as he leaned deliberately forwards and banged on the desk.

"When I order something, it is an order, and it is done, Miss Arthur. Please to understand that now and in the future."

"Yes, sir . . . yes, Mr. Saxby."

He gave a slight groan, but she saw it was not entirely because of her impudence but because of the long wearying morning.

"All delicate souls?" she asked with wry sympathy, and borrowing from Bill Bethel. "All gossamer? Fragility? Anything but flesh and blood, snub noses and freckles?"

"Mostly," he agreed. "Thompson can't wear wool near the skin and Wilkins can't eat strawberries."

"We don't have many strawberries," Sophie put in

73

mildly.

"Radcliffe can take baths but not showers. Withers can take showers but not baths. Green has an allergy for cats. Oh, for one, just one, ordinary, uninhibited, un-allergic, insensitive male minor!"

"They'll all be that in a month," assured Sophie. She added : "I mean, the girls were."

"I expect so," he conceded, "and I expect, too, it's only for once. Those parents today were the new parents of the new boys. It's either the desolation of their children leaving home for the initial time that turns them into clucking mammas, or the heady intoxication of being without the young demons for a while giving them a side-effect guilt complex and making them extra fussy before they kick up their heels at being gloriously unencompassed again."

"Don't you like them?" she asked.

"The mothers? On the contrary. There were several stunning beauties today."

"I meant the boys."

"Would I be doing what I am doing if I didn't?"

"But what are you doing, Mr. Saxby? I mean— well, you're not really a Headmaster, are you?"

He looked at her closely. "I'm in Education," he said formally.

"The book part of it," she pointed out.

"You think that's a different cup of tea, I take it."

"Very different." She was pleased she had got that in. She sat blissfully back.

He did not speak for a long moment, and as she waited Sophie's pleasure began to diminish somewhat. She kept her eyes off him, off the firm male fingers tapping speculatively together. Speculating about her, no doubt.

"You are a small feline, aren't you?" he said at last. "I was right about your taste of cream last night."

74

"What, Headmaster?"

"After you had met Bill Bethel I remarked upon it, remember? All your satisfaction showed. No doubt he had been flattering you. Now, to clinch my case, your claws are showing." A pause. "Against me."

"Did you send for me to tell me this?" Sophie asked.

"I sent for you some forty minutes ago to assist me with the parents. The parents are now long departed."

"I told you I was busy."

"And I told you I observed you." He waited a moment. "Conferring with our gym master."

"Naturally. I also conferred with the Nab—with the house director."

"And will also confer tomorrow with the maths, science, English and geography teachers."

"Yes, Mr. Saxby."

"Good," he awarded. "Nothing like an amiable staff for a contented school."

"So you've heard," she suggested outrageously, "or been told."

"Observed," he corrected quite calmly, but his lips were tight. "When," he asked, "are you going to call off your dogs, Miss Arthur?"

"My dogs?" she queried.

"Finish my persecution."

"You? Persecuted?"

"Yes. When are you going to call a halt?"

She had not expected that, and for a few moments she was discountenanced.

"I'm sorry," she actually brought herself to say. "I suppose I have harped."

"You have," he assured her.

"But I can't help myself, I can't stop still feeling resentful for Father."

"You mean for Father's daughter," he corrected

thinly.

She did not answer.

"However, we've gone through all this," he went on, "and repetition will get us nowhere."

"My father is nowhere now."

"Miss Arthur, *will you stop all this*!" His voice, loudly raised, had such a sharp edge to it that Sophie visibly flinched. She also obeyed.

"I'm sorry I was not here in time to assist you," she told him presently in a quiet voice. "It won't happen in the future. I promise you that then I'll leave whatever I'm doing and come at once. Seeing I've failed you in that, is there anything I can do now?"

"Yes. Leave," he said wearily.

Sophie started to do so, but she only got to the door.

"Miss Arthur," he called.

"Yes, Mr. Saxby?"

"Tomorrow we have an entirely different intake."

"Yes, the senior school."

"There will be no new enrolments, or at least very few, so no parental sessions like today."

"You'll be glad of that."

"Yes. However, replanting boys of thirteen to seventeen will need even more attention. Or should I say—inattention?" A significant pause. "From you."

"Please?"

"You are by far the most junior mistress here, and not unattractive."

"Thank you," she smiled.

"Boys of thirteen to seventeen might even say attractive."

"Thank you again."

"No, thank the boys, or rather the age group in which they find themselves."

"Oh, I will, Headmaster."

"But let it stop at that. At thanks. Make your attention really inattention. You follow me?"

She did, and she stared incredulously at him, then changed the stare to a glare.

He was unmoved, though. He simply shrugged and said: "It happens with monotonous regularity. Where the small boy looks around for a mother figure, the young man looks round for a different figure altogether."

"This is in very bad taste, Headmaster."

"It is also very true. Books have had it as themes many times. Plays have."

"So you want my promise now not to speak to the older intake."

"Don't be ridiculous, you know I don't mean that."

"Then if you meant not encouraging them, why didn't you say so?"

"Because I didn't mean non-encouragement either. I meant . . . well . . . oh, dammit! You're a nice-looking young girl and the older teenagers soon become aware of that. What I'm trying to tell you, Miss Arthur, is that *you* should be aware of it in advance."

"You mean be neck to knee in whatever I wear, scoop my hair and put on hornrimmed glasses?"

"I mean treat them as you would treat a brother, had you one, and by heaven, why haven't you one? Why haven't you at least a sister? You're the most spoiled rotten only child that a man could have happen to him. All I can say is 'Poor Arthur.' "

"Yes," she agreed bitterly, "poor Arthur." She waited. "Is that all?"

"For the moment, yes."

She did not wait for the next moment, she hurried through the door.

She wondered how Father had fared in the influx, and went looking for him. Yesterday there had been talk of bringing him downstairs to do the enrolments,

77

but in the preparation for the arrival and then the arrival of the boys, Sophie had not found time to check. Afterwards, she grimaced, there had been a summons from the Headmaster.—"When I order something, it's an order, and it's done, Miss Arthur."

"Have you seen Father?" she asked one of the mistresses.

"Mr. Headmistress . . . Mr. Arthur did the new enrolments. Because Headmaster wished to interview the parents, Mr. Arthur was put in the seniors' room."

"Thanks, Faith." Sophie went down the passage.

Because it was the advanced classroom and not a private office, Sophie did not knock, but simply entered. She was rather surprised to see her father moving, if clumsily, though the bandaging would see to that, across the room. Mr. Arthur looked surprised, too.

"I thought you were with Mr. Saxby, dear."

"Is that why you're sneaking around?" Sophie laughed.

"It is awkward to remain in the one place, and as you can see I'm perfectly capable of hobbling."

"Did you do the enrolments?"

"Every one of them," he said proudly.

"Then the Board—and Headmaster—need not worry about the Arthurs being a dead loss."

"I'm sure they wouldn't, anyhow," refused Mr. Arthur, but Sophie did not add her agreement. After he had hobbled back to his chair she came and perched on a desk beside him.

"Was it different from enrolling girls?"

"Yes. John instead of Alice, William instead of Mary. No, Sophie, it was much the same."

"Tomorrow you'll have the seniors. Father, how do you really think it will go?"

"The same as today. Enrolments, junior or senior,

are much the same."

"I mean the new system."

"It should have been the old system," Mr. Arthur said, "then you wouldn't be wondering now. Both sexes should mingle right from the cradle."

"Headmaster thinks the same. He thinks you should have had a son."

"I rather think he said you should have had a brother," deduced Mr. Arthur shrewdly, "or a sister. Someone to prevent you from being what you are."

"A spoiled only child. Am I, dear?"

"If you are, I've done it."

"But am I?"

"No."

"Thank you, Father." There was one of those companionable silences that the two of them often had.

Sophie broke it.

"Estrella is the only one worrying me."

"That pretty redhead?"

"Ah, you've noticed, too."

"You would have to notice Estrella. But why are you worrying?"

"Pictures in the inside of her wardrobe, at the back of her bed, on her desk, inside her cupboards."

"Family ones?" asked Mr. Arthur with a laugh.

"Pop group idols, a few movie stars, T.V. heroes."

"I wouldn't think any more about it, she's hardly likely to notice a mere pimply senior after Gary Cooper."

"After who?"

"Sorry, Sophie, I'm twenty years out. Who is it now?"

"By the time I tell you he'll be finished, too," Sophie smiled.

"Then why the concern?"

"Estrella's one of those girls whose nose *isn't* forever

in a book."

"Then dismiss her from your anxious thoughts.
Now, Virginia is much more likely."

"Our scholastic pride and joy?"

"Exactly, Sophie. One day Virginia will look up
from her Greek mythology and see a god much more
to her liking."

"So long as he doesn't see her, though according to
Headmaster, I will be the focus, being the youngest on
the staff, and, to a boy's undemanding eyes, not unattractive. Father, it isn't a laughing matter."

"It's hilarious." Mr. Arthur dried his eyes. "It's also
a timely warning, Sophie."

"Not to encourage them? As though I would! As
though I need to be told!"

"Wise of the Headmaster, though."

Sophie looked obliquely at her father. "He isn't,
you know."

"Sophie!"

"He isn't that," she insisted.

"Headmaster? No, he's so high on the association
board you could say he runs it."

"Top brass," nodded Sophie, "cream of the cream.
But still not a teacher." She would have gone further,
but there was a certain look on her father's face that
warned her off. "If you've finished, Mr. Arthur," she
said instead, "and want to go upstairs again, I'll tell
our men."

"Yes, dear, do that. And Sophie—"

Sophie waited.

"Nothing," he smiled at her.

"I know," she read from him, "I'll call off the
dogs."

"What, dear?"

"I'll call a halt, Father."

"Yes, please, Sophie." He watched her go out to

round up the gardener and janitor.

That night was the first co-ed meal at Apa, and it did not go off without a few incidents. However, that was expected; even first meals after vacations did not go off smoothly, even when the sex was only one type. Now it was two. Two *opposing* sexes at this age, it appeared.

The boys started it . . . or did they? The girls declared the boys started it by landing a marble fair and square into Irene's bowl of soup, but the boys said that Irene, passing the soup down the table, started it by bumping the soup over Kevin's knees.

Irene's squeals of agony were enough to set the girls accusing the boys of scalding her to death. (Kevin was ignored.) The death accusation suggested something to Irene. She slipped convincingly from the table and became a dead figure on the floor. An alert male of nine called Michael leapt up and began mouth-to-mouth resuscitation, only Irene recovered quickly, screaming now that she was being bitten to death.

"I was only blowing in life," objected Michael, "and besides, she was only pretending to be dead."

Irene took up her deathly pose again, and Julian, an angel-faced ten, took the flowers from the vase on the table and placed them on her breast.

"Two minutes' silence," he called . . . the silence part being mouthed as he, and Michael, were marched by the headmaster out of the dining-room. Irene, for her punishment, was told to remain where she was. Sophie, at whose table all the trouble seemed to be centred, stopped Jane from feeding her spoons of jelly.

"But she'll die of hunger," appealed Jane.

"She's already been scalded and bitten to death, so I scarcely think this can do much worse."

At last the meal was over and the children were

released.

"All the supervisors please assemble in the staff eating section," called Garrick Saxby. "I more or less anticipated a beginning like this, so I instructed our cook to hold some dinner back. I scarcely think any of you have had an enjoyable meal."

There were murmurs of pleased agreement as those who had been on roster tailed the Head to a more elegant repast. Sophie, who felt she had had enough for one session, and was not hungry, anyway, decided not to go.

"That included you, Miss Arthur," Garrick Saxby called without turning. The man, she thought, must have eyes at the back of his head.

She tagged on with the rest.

There were appreciative murmurs as the staff who had sat with the school and only turned over their food now sat and ate their food.

"It will be better next time," encouraged Saxby of the initial school meal, "and in a month's time . . ." He turned his large palms upward in a cheerful gesture. He asked had anyone any suggestions.

"None," said Faith Prentice busily. "I think you managed it very well, Headmaster."

"Admirably," said one of the new male staff to whom Sophie had been introduced but whose name now she could not remember.

"Miss Arthur?" asked Garrick Saxby down the table, and Sophie realized that her lack of praise had not gone unnoticed.

"I think your mistake was—" Now Sophie paused, realizing too late that she could have worded what she had to say much better.

"Yes, Miss Arthur?"

"That perhaps we should not have eaten en famille."

"In a family? Both sexes together as it would happen in a family?"

"Yes."

"And that was my mistake?" The faintest emphasis on "my".

"Yes."

"You don't go along with families? Being an only child yourself I expect that could be so." He smiled at her.

"I really meant," Sophie mumbled, "until we got established."

"There's no 'getting' established, Miss Arthur, we're one at once."

"I agree with you, Headmaster," said two of the women teachers together, "start off as you intend to continue."

"With marbles in the soup."—Oh dear, thought Sophie, but too late again, what has got into me?

She only toyed with her food. The others, who naturally enough had lost their appetite in the far from equable meal conditions they had just supervised, ate with relish. Every bit choked Sophie.

She wondered what other torment she would be asked to undergo, but to her surprise and relief it stopped at that.

"Thank you all so much for your co-operation," said Garrick Saxby, and smiling at them he also nodded their dismissal.

"What a man!" one of the women admired to one of the male teachers. "I'm sure we'll be vastly improved at each meal, don't you?"

Sophie was glad the question was not directed at her. She saw Bill Bethel apparently waiting for her at the door, and deliberately went across. She was now off duty, so could do so. Father, too, had been taken upstairs, his meal taken after him, so she would not be needed there. Also . . . and the real reason, even though she liked Bill Bethel instinctively and was looking forward to a talk with him . . . *the Headmaster was not going to be pleased.* He had said that an amiable staff made for an amiable school, but he had implied at the same time (for Sophie, anyway) that the amiability should stop at that. Certainly he had not envisaged one of his female staff stepping into the scented mountain air with one of his male staff, then crossing to a fragrant . . . and dark . . . garden. No, never that, Mr. 'Headmaster' Saxby.

Bill put the tips of his fingers under Sophie's arm as the dark garden turned into an even darker corner. Sophie knew the plots and beds by heart and could have walked in the blackest midnight, but the feel of Bill's fingers, she found, was quite pleasant. Bill Bethel was pleasing himself.

"You weren't very impressed with our first meal," Bill said, "but be fair, it was only a beginning."

Sophie could have answered that it was not the meal but the Headmaster, but she decided to take the easy way and agree. "I expect it is early," she said.

"After tomorrow we can really get into our stride, Miss Arthur.—Look, Miss Arthur is all right in front of the kids, but does it have to be that between ourselves?"

"No, Bill."

"Thanks, Sophie. It is Sophie?"

"Yes."

"I like it," he said boyishly.

"I like William, it's a basic name, not like—well, the Headmaster's."

"That's an old name, too, Sophie. Garrick means mighty warrior."

Sophie grimaced in the dark.

Because he did not see the grimace, Bill went blithely on. "He's a great guy . . . the things he's suggested for both of us."

"Both of us?" she queried.

"Both sides of the co-ed."

"The Headmaster has?"

"Things I wouldn't have thought of," nodded Bill. "Ballroom dancing, for instance."

"What?"

"That's where you come in. I come in with you, too, you have to have a partner, but it will be really your thing, Sophie."

Sophie said incredulously and slangily: "Oh, come off it. Kids don't dance these days, they just get up and express their feeling in movement. They'd laugh their heads off. In fact our girls do now if they see it in a T.V. movie."

"Ah, but comes the time when they need a foxtrot up their sleeve. Or, as Headmaster said, the know-how of the bridal waltz."

"Is he marrying them off already?"

"It's just forward thinking," said Bill. "Another need for you, and again we have to thank Headmaster, is teaching the boys the jig and the fling."

"What?" gasped Sophie again.

"Originally they're men's dances," Bill explained. "An Irish Jig done properly is as male as a Russian cossack turn, and the fling becomes a pre-battle warm-up."

"I doubt if I can produce those results, but I can teach the basic steps. What do you intend to provide for the girls in their turn?"

"Better gym methods . . . also I was watching some of your basketball hopes trying to throw goals and they were lousy. Oh, yes, Sophie, as Headmaster said, I think we'll complement each other."

"Did he now?" That was decidedly unexpected, Sophie thought, after his barely-veiled warning to her.

They walked back to the school. There were voices in the staff room, bright, exhilarated voices, male tones among them. One male tone in particular. Bill turned instinctively to join them.

"I'm not coming," Sophie told him.

"On duty?" he sympathized.

"Yes, my night to help Matron."

"Oh, tough luck. Our own Nabob is a marvel, has the kids bathed and bedded before you can turn round. Never needs a hand. Come down, won't you, when you're free."

"Of course," promised Sophie falsely, and went upstairs to Honor's suite, because she was *not* on duty, and would *not* be coming down. Not to pay homage to that voice.

The enrolment the next day was much simpler. All but a few of the senior boys were the old Kingsley scholars, and it was only a matter of writing their names up in a new register. No interviewing of parents to learn of allergies such as wool next the skin or strawberries, these problems had been ironed out years ago.

The younger section of the senior boys looked with unconcealed battle in their eyes on the enemy, the enemy being their contemporary girls around the Fourth Grade. The older boys eyed the girls quite differently, though not the younger ones, whom, Sophie suspected, they did not even see, but the top classes.

Estrella was in her element. She knew she was the prettiest and enjoyed the long looks, but, just as Father had said, after Gary Cooper . . . oh, goodness, she was saying it now . . . seventeen-year-olders just didn't add up.

However, Virginia, Sophie noted with satisfaction, did not react as Mr. Arthur had warned, so Father was not infallible. Bookish Virginia did not even look up from her mythology at the newcomers.

Someone was doing more than his share of looking, though, Sophie noted. Looking at her. It was one of the two new boys. Timothy Wylie would be no trouble. He had a twin sister at Apa, so his parents had snatched the opportunity of educating the pair together, but the other boy, Rodney, at the age of seventeen was only just starting school. He came, Bill told Sophie, from a remote island near Fiji, and had been educated by correspondence.

"He's to do his final exams here, then go on to University. It's a bit hard for these kids in outlandish places. It's not so easy to catch up."

Sophie knew that Bill did not mean just in education. She felt a little unhappy about Rodney already. She felt she knew in advance what the next few weeks were going to be like for him. The boy was homesick, yet like many homesick victims of his years not so nostalgic for a comforting mother figure but a younger, livelier figure. Not, as the Headmaster had said, 'unattractive.' For herself, Sophie was not worrying, she knew she could deal with boys like Rodney. But she knew, too, that Garrick Saxby would be watching her methods of dealing, watching her every move, and that annoyed her.

She mingled with the other teachers around the intake, accepting the wolf whistles the boys gave her whenever a master was not in earshot . . . but trying at the same time not to be too close to Rodney. It was hard, however; Rodney was determined to be close to her. When there was one very distinct whistle, and Rodney was near, the tall, thin, good-looking young man said :

87

"Disgusting, aren't they, Miss Arthur?"

"Oh, I don't know, Rodney. It is Rodney, isn't it?"

"Yes."

"It's just a phase, Rodney."

"I don't think I would have a phase like that."

"Well, perhaps it's been different for you."

"Oh, it has, Miss Arthur. Your name is Sophie, isn't it?"

"Yes, but I hardly think—"

"Oh, I wasn't dreaming of calling you that, I just wanted to know. It's a very beautiful name, Sophia. Has it a meaning? I know it's in history, I've read it in the family tree of European kings and queens. But is there a meaning?"

"I'm told it means Wisdom, Rodney."

Rodney seemed a little disappointed, and looked also about to tell his own version, so Sophie said quickly: "So you're interested in history?"

"Yes. I like all my studies. Not Maths so much, but—"

"Mythology?"

"Oh, very much."

"So does Virginia, that pretty dark-haired senior over there." As she said it Sophie felt guilty, but she just had to foist Rodney off before he got any further. She thought briefly, and uncertainly, of Garrick Saxby and what he would think of such an evasion; best, she knew, to say right now:

"Before you start, Rodney, *don't*," than to try to divert him in such a dangerous way. But Sophie had never been very good at discouraging people, denouncing them . . . unless, and she realized it with surprise, it was the headmaster.

She need not have concerned herself about Virginia, for Rodney did not even glance at her.

"How do you like sport, Rodney?" Sophie asked a

little desperately.

Rodney grimaced.

"Yet you must take it, of course."

"I don't see why . . . I mean, not dished out to you as it appears to be dished out in schools."

"You've never been to school before?"

"My mother taught me from mainland correspondence lessons. Our island is on the equator, Miss Arthur, one end of it is today and the other end is tomorrow. The date line goes through it."

"How interesting, Rodney, you could have two birthdays." Sophie thought she had better concentrate on sport, for undoubtedly, like it or not, Rodney would be expected to participate. Also sport was safer.

"I can see why team efforts would confuse you," she sympathized. "I guess you have to start early for a football or cricket side. But there's gymnasium work."

"The things they do I did unthinkingly in our coconut trees," said Rodney contemptuously.

"On the coast Kingsley still has a boat shed," Sophie tried next.

"I have my own outrigger," Rodney demeaned.

"Well, I'm sure in time . . ." hoped Sophie, but she was not sure at all. Nor in any given time. She gave Rodney an uncertain smile, uncertain since she did not know how he would take the smile, rate it, but you just couldn't scowl at the boy.

She moved away, and soon found Estrella beside her.

"A load of creeps, aren't they?" patronized the school belle.

Thank heaven at least for that, thought Sophie. Aloud she said: "They can't all be Gary Coopers, dear," then thought how silly she was to say such a thing to a sixteen-year-old.

89

"Gary Cooper! He was bee-utiful," enthused Estrella. "My mother had him in her scrapbook. I adore mature men, Miss Arthur. Miss Arthur, have you ever looked secretly at the Headmaster?"

"Secretly, Estrella?"

"When he's not looking at you."

"Yes, I have."

"Isn't he a dish?"

"Well—er—" Sophie began to mingle again.

The dinner that night went off much smoother than the first night. They all ate en famille, and would continue eating like that even if a riot began, Sophie knew, perish the thought of *that* man taking her advice. But Mr. Saxby did select what he considered were the trouble spots, and he put them at a table topped and bottomed by the Nabob and Matron, or, if you were a liberal, by Matron and the Nabob, since the table went either way. The Nabob, Sophie had learned from Bill, could control the worst riot with a flick of his eyelashes, and no girl yet had taken Matron for a ride. So all went well.

Again Sophie was not rostered, so she went out to the garden. In case Bill might think she made a habit of this, and join her, and that fact come to the knowledge of Headmaster Saxby, Sophie passed through the garden and went down the drive.

It was not quite dark, only a deep pansy blue. Standing by the big gates, Sophie had a feeling of something different somehow, and she looked around. Not the mountains, they were eternally the same, but—

Why, it was their sign! Instead of Apa School for Girls it was Apa-Kingsley Co-ed. Nice of Garrick Saxby, anyway, to put the girls first!

Underneath there were two mottos, their own *Ne cede malis*, Yield not to misfortune, and a new *Facta non verba* . . .

"Deeds, not words," said a voice.

Sophie looked through the gathering darkness to the Headmaster.

"Is that your motto?" she asked.

"Ours now."

"But ours is—"

"Yes, and that one is ours, too. We are one, Miss Arthur. That's what co-ed means."

"I prefer Yield not to misfortune," Sophie said stiffly.

"I wouldn't argue about that," he nodded, "for you certainly practise it."

"Just because I'm loyal to Father—"

"An odd loyalty, surely, haranguing but doing nothing constructive. That brings us to the next motto, Deeds, not words. How about fewer words, Miss Arthur?"

"And more deeds?" she said impudently.

"That part of the motto calls for strict discipline. It also depends on what deeds you plan. It refers, too, to other things. For instance, watch yourself with young Rodney Berthold."

"Rodney?" she queried.

"I saw you two talking today. I am now ordering less tea and sympathy there."

"I always make it cocoa and the radiogram," Sophie said smartly, "you're a few decades out."

"But then I'm two decades older."

"Are you forty?"

"Getting there," he shrugged. "Tell me," he said quite unexpectedly, "does that seem like Methuselah to you?"

"No," she answered.

"But in comparison to—say, Bill Bethel?"

"Yes," she answered now. Then she asked, "Why?"

"Just idle questioning."

"I can't believe that, I can't believe anything you do would be idle."

"Do I seem so grim?" he asked.

"Perhaps not grim, but certainly set to do what you intend to do."

"Is that bad?"

"I'm sure it's good, only——"

"Only, Miss Arthur?"

"Only not everything can be dictated. A heart can't be told."

There was a pause, then he asked almost conversationally: "You don't like me, do you?"

"I haven't really thought about it," she endeavoured to elude.

"You don't like me." He ignored her effort of evasion.

"No." If he asked for frankness then he could have it.

"I think that's the first time you've been honest," he told her. "All this outcry for your father has only been on behalf of your father's daughter."

"You told me so several times before," she flashed.

"A teacher's burden," he shrugged, "repeating the lesson. You should know that."

"But then I'm not really a teacher, I'm only on approval."

"Also," he went on, "I'm not really a teacher, either, as you've told me."

"Yet scarcely on approval."

He ignored that.

"So," he concluded, "we're both more or less in the same category."

"You more, me less."

She felt the cool tips of his fingers under her elbow. "Time to go back," he said.

"I don't want to go back yet."

"Nonetheless you will do so. If it's good enough for him, for our gym master, then it's good enough for me."

"What's good enough?"

"Walking in the dark. Loitering. Dallying."

"We didn't!" Sophie protested.

"No? But who is there to say that about us?"

"Mr. Saxby, you would be the—"

"The last one," he finished before Sophie could. "So let's not give an impression to the contrary, Miss Arthur. Let's return at once. Are you going to join the others in the staff room?"

"I'm going to join Father."

"So am I, I haven't had an opportunity to speak to Mr. Arthur all day."

"Then I'll leave you to it and have an early night."

"Don't on my account."

"On my account," she said stolidly, and, after opening the door of Honor's suite, she had a few words with her father, then went along to her room.

She could hear Garrick Saxby, on Father's instructions, finding the decanter and glasses. Downstairs she could hear the staff chattering and laughing. It was quite early, a long night stretched in front of her, and she felt restless and a little frustrated.

She went to the window to look out, always up on the mountain it soothed her to look out. But this time she withdrew at once.

Rodney. In the garden directly beneath the window. Rodney picking a flower and holding it as though he was going to throw it. Up.

Sophie extinguished the light and prepared herself for a long, boring night.

CHAPTER FIVE

You would not have credited that everything could have settled down so easily, so smoothly. The next day the individual school records were taken out, scrutinized and assessed, classes formulated, rooms assigned, teachers appointed, children placed at their desks. No boys strictly to the left side of the room, girls strictly to the right side (or vice versa) but rather where they naturally and instinctively found themselves, and even at the desks, built as they were for two, both sexes sitting down equally. Here at Apa-Kingsley it appeared that the only segregation was to be in the houses at night.

After a mild epidemic of giggles in the junior section, plus a pulling of hair and a throwing of various missiles, after a few fluttering eyes and some romantic notes in the senior school, it was as though it had always been like this: just young men and young women simply being together. Male and female (junior variety) created He them.

That dealt with the scholastic side, but what about the play hours *out* of the schoolrooms? Sophie wondered a little dubiously. Also the hours during school hours that were formally appointed for physical education. For these significant moments she could only hope for something less than abject failure. She certainly dared not dream of success.

But her first Irish Jig and Highland Reel lessons with the intermediate boys went off amazingly well.

The recordings she selected were bright and tappy, and soon all the class, whatever their forebears, were learning the basic national steps. Angus Anderson, whose junior brother had previously been indicated by Bill to Sophie as Trouble, refused both (proving that Trouble ran in the family) unless some corroboree steps were included. His great-great-great-great-grandfather, he announced, not batting an eyelid above a Scottish blue eye, had been Bennelong, that famous aboriginal chief.

"You must be proud," applauded Sophie, "and I'm pleased to tell you that we do have an aboriginal record."

"With a didgeridoo?"

"Yes."

"Is it a war dance?"

"Yes."

"Then no go. I'm strictly a pacificist." Angus looked beatifically . . . and wickedly . . . at Sophie.

"You're also an impossible boy," said Sophie sternly. "Now get into the Jig line at once."

"Jig, with a name of Angus Anderson!" sniffed Anderson.

"I thought it was Bennelong."

"While he thinks out his family tree *in my study* just go ahead with the Jig, Miss Arthur." The Headmaster had come into the gym, and the troublemaker did not look so pleased with himself.

Bill Bethel meanwhile got on very well with the girls; a male tutor, conceded Sophie, was far more suitable for ambitious gymnasts when it came to helping them over the horse, or for settling basketball or hockey disputes, than a female.

When the mutual study was nature study, Bill and Sophie took the classes together into the bush, along with chops to grill on green sticks and potatoes to

95

throw in the fire's embers. Both male and female, young, and not as young, thoroughly enjoyed that.

The ballroom lessons, Sophie learned, were to be taken together. The instruction was "offered" the school at first, then when no applicants applied, they were *told* to attend. Sheepishly, but well aware already that what the Head said went, both sexes did attend.

The dances by compulsion were happy enough in the modern numbers, their participants standing their several yards apart and expressing themselves to a beat their generation understood, but when the intricacies of the waltz were introduced, it all became sheer torture. It was all very well to flutter eyelids, it seemed, exchange notes, but to stand up and actually encircle the girl's waist was downright ludicrous.

"Closer," yelled Bill, running up and down the columns of partners, "she won't bite you!" He addressed himself to the boys.

The boys looked as though they didn't quite believe this . . . but the girls looked as though they knew something else. *And would.* The music began, but, in spite of the foot pattern Sophie had drawn on the blackboard, no one moved an inch.

"One-two-three," called Bill Bethel desperately.

"I think," proposed Sophie, "we should have started with the Gipsy Tap or even a foxtrot, something with more spirit and less dreaminess, then come more gradually to this."

"Nonsense," said Garrick Saxby, standing in the wings as it were, "the waltz is the greatest of all dances, it's essential that they know it."

"In this latter twentieth century?" disbelieved Sophie.

"I would say in as many centuries as you can count in the future, Miss Arthur."

Tartly Sophie demanded: "And can *you* waltz?"

"Can *you*?"

"Naturally, since I'm the phys ed mistress." That was rather putting herself forward for a certain sarcastic reminder, and Sophie waited for it.

"That was not what I asked," Garrick Saxby said instead of what she had thought he would say, "I asked could you waltz?"

"Yes."

"I don't mean your modern jazz waltz, I mean waltz."

"Yes" she said again.

"Prove it," he ordered.

"Prove it?" She stared at him incredulously. "I would look a fool gyrating round and round by myself. Or did you intend to provide me with a cushion? Our dancing teacher used to do that, we always danced with a cushion."

"Couldn't you find yourself a partner, then?"

"Miss Phipps wanted us all to learn the girl's steps, not the boy's, and we were not then co-ed."

"Would you like a cushion now?"

"Of course not."

"Then it will have to be me, I'm afraid."

"You?" she echoed.

"I told you I waltzed."

"Yes, but—"

"Bill is instructing, so he's out, and there are no other male teachers present. Our boys are noticeably unco-operative. So I—or the cushion?"

"You," she said unenthusiastically, and was glad by his prompt answer that her tonelessness had shown.

"Thanks for the warm anticipation," he awarded coldly. He held out his arms and unwillingly she went to them.

"Class," he called, "this is how a waltz should look when at last you find it in you to move away from where you have apparently taken root. Right, Mr. Bethel, the Blue Danube side, please."

The waltz began.

The fingers of one of his hands touched the fingers of one of Sophie's hands, she felt his other hand round her waist. She clutched the large shoulder above her own shoulder with her spare hand. They stood a correct several inches apart. At first. It was all very formal, perfectly disciplined, completely impersonal as an authentic waltz should be. So what happened? Why did Sopie begin to feel as she did feel? *In*formal? *Un*disciplined?—Personal?

The strains quickened. Their steps quickened. Sophie knew her blood quickened. It's the tune, she thought a little wildly, I always loved the Blue Danube, and I've always loved moving to its notes. It's an intoxicating theme. I—I'm intoxicated.

Garrick Saxby began to rotate.

Round and round they went. They could have been a clockwork couple wound up by a key, they moved so rhythmically, so together. Fleetingly, as they whirled, Sophie saw Bill Bethel's rueful face. Also Rodney's shut-in one. Oh, dear, she began to think, oh, dear . . . then she thought of nothing, she simply abandoned herself to music, to movement, to a man's encircling arms. Garrick Saxby's arms.

He was rotating her anti-clockwise now, unwinding her so she would not emerge at the fast approaching end of the waltz confused and giddy.

"*Not* Sophie," he said softly but distinctly in her ear.

"Not Sophie?" she echoed.

"Sophia means Wisdom. Did you know that? But you're not wise, or you wouldn't have danced this waltz with me. Can't you see, you unwise one, that now you're committed?"

98

"Committed?" She tried to look up at him, but it was hard, for the unwinding was augmenting and she could not keep him in focus.

"Committed, Miss Headmistress," he bantered, and before she could retort the dance came to an end. He gave a final whirl, held her firmly as she gained her balance, then they both took a bow together.

"I'll try that," called one of the boys at once.

"I'll partner you," offered a girl. Steps began round the room, awkward steps a first, a little embarrassed, but the ice was broken.

Only four people did not look delighted with what had happened. Garrick Saxby looked slightly bored, Sophie looked a little bewildered, Bill Bethel plainly envious now as well as rueful, and Rodney—Rodney did not look anything, for Rodney had simply gone out of the gymnasium.

If the Head noticed Rodney's absence, he made no comment, but Bill Bethel told Sophie the next day that Mr. Saxby had told him that if Rodney was not inclined yet to join in anything, take his part in any of the various teams, at least he must get some physical exercise down at the beach, or on the old Kingsley rowboat that was still kept in the Nerang River shed. Bill added that Rodney had agreed to take out the boat.

"Alone?" Sophie asked.

"Rowing is not an exercise that requires a team."

"I suppose so. So long as he does what's required of him and just doesn't row round a corner and sit."

"He appeared quite keen," Bill told her.

When Rodney came to Sophie later that day and asked her to go with him to the river tomorrow she hardly thought she could refuse. The boy had been ordered exercise, and if he would only exercise with someone with him, then she felt it her duty to concede

99

. . . this once.

"This once, Rodney," she stipulated, "for the reason that I know the Nerang River, and you don't, that I can tell you where, and where you should not, row. It's quite easy, too, to get yourself lost in that maze of canals and quays. Of course you'd emerge some time, but it can be a puzzle."

"Yes," said Rodney.

"It happens, too," continued Sophie, "that I have to go down to the coast, anyway, so that's another reason why I'll agree to come. But in the future if you don't wish to row alone, then you must take one of your friends."

"I haven't any."

"Then make some."

"They've all been together for years, Soph—Miss Arthur, I'm the only newchum."

"It should be all the more rewarding getting a friend, then."

"Rewarding?" disparaged Rodney.

"There are some fine boys here," defended Sophie.

"Not as fine as the boys back on Fini."

"Was that your island?"

"Yes. My parents have a plantation there. Oh, Soph—Miss Arthur, I do miss it all abominably."

"I'm sure you do, dear, but I'm sure, too, the feeling will pass. Especially if you work out your misgiving at the end of a pair of oars."

". . . Yes," agreed Rodney after a distinct pause, and Sophie put the hesitancy down to Rodney's doubt as to the truth in this, the sense of working out homesickness by rowing round a river, but the next day down at Surfers' Paradise, her shopping done, and now round at the old Kingsley boathouse to be duly rowed by Rodney. Sophie saw that Rodney's hesitancy had not been concerned with theory but with actuality. The actuality of an engine and not oars. Rodney sat in a trim, inboard craft.

"Rodney!" she gasped.

"It's quite all right, So—Miss Arthur, I've handled boats all my life, you'll be quite safe in this."

"But, Rodney dear, I hardly think this was what the Head had in mind when he ordered you to exercise."

"There's more exercise than you'd think manipulating these things."

"But, Rodney, you shouldn't have."

"I was told to get into the fresh air and I chose to do so this way. After all, it's no money out of the school's exchequer, I'm paying for the hire myself."— Yes, thought Sophie, that would be true, Rodney was never short of money.

"When I told you I'd come," she said with misgiving, "I thought you would be rowing, Rodney, and I intended to tell you which quays were too shallow and which were all right. Some of the newer ones are a little short of water still, and you could run on to a mudbank."

"I'll need that information all the more now," Rodney pointed out reasonably. "Do please get in, Miss Arthur."

"I really don't know what to do," frowned Sophie. "You've deceived me, Rodney."

"I won't ever again. I thought it would save time this way. I thought you could show me the whole thing in one go, Miss Arthur, instead of taking the afternoon to sneak up some little canal. Which it would take if I had to manoeuvre around manually."

"That makes sense," agreed Sophie. "All right then, Rodney, but you must promise me that next time—"

"Next time I'll row every inch of the way," Rodney assured her. "I'm good at that, too. Good at all water

101

stuff. I don't know a thing about football, nor cricket, and my tennis was spasmodic, I only played it when I crossed the island to another plantation. But the sea, that was my love." He sighed. "Outboard, inboard, skiing, simply rowing as you wanted me to, but best of all sailing. Miss Arthur, there's nothing like a sail, you know." As he said it Rodney rather contemptuously kicked off the engine and the craft moved forward.

He was competent, there was no denying that. He also obeyed Sophie when she shook her head over a narrow quay, over too-shallow a way under a culvert. She found herself beginning to enjoy the outing, delighting in the smooth green water matched by the smooth green lawns of the palatial canalside villas with their jetties and marinas gay with bobbing craft, but looking at Rodney she saw he was not so amused. In fact he looked frustrated.

He caught her glance and shrugged. "I just like it a little more free, Miss Arthur, these afternoon jaunts close me in somehow." He looked eagerly at her. "Do you think we could let ourselves out a bit?"

"What do you mean, Rodney?"

"Leave the quays . . . go up the broadwater."

"Oh, no, dear."

"Just a bit of a way before we go back," pleaded Rodney. "Please, Soph— Miss Arthur, there's no sea smell here."

Sophie could sympathize with him there. She remembered going out once with Father and Honor, she recalled that tang of salt and seaweed, that feeling of utter, ungirt abandonment.

"Please. Just for five minutes." Rodney looked at her wistfully.

"Oh, very well then, along the broadwater."

Rodney accelerated the engine at once; it was quite

a powerful engine, and he must have paid a high hiring fee. He turned the craft in an arc, then they spun along the broadwater past Southport, then past Labrador.

"Enough, Rodney!" Sophie called.

He looked back at her with shining eyes. Poor boy, she thought with a pang, it must be so different for him over here, so confined after Fini Island.

"Back," she ordered again, but not quite so definitely this time. And Rodney took advantage of that softening. He pushed the engine to its full extent, pushed the craft in an outward direction. Outward bound, not in.

"Rodney," called Sophie, not indefinite now, seeing his purpose too late. "Rodney, stop!"

Rodney kept on.

Angler's Paradise was left behind, Hollywell, Hope Island, Jacob's Well. On their right, to the east, the tip of South Stradbroke Island was coming up, and, just as though he knew it as the locals did, Rodney was turning the craft through Tippler's Passage, out to the sea. Not a rough sea, it was seldom that, there were too many protective islands for that sort of danger, but treacherous because of its sudden shallows and its eastern currents. It was said you could paddle up to Brisbane in complete safety *if you knew where*. Rodney had been lucky so far, but he still didn't know *where*, and his luck might not hold.

"Rodney!" she tried again.

But it appeared Rodney's luck was holding, the boat was responding magnificently, and Rodney was perfectly relaxed behind the wheel. No doubt all would have gone well, too, Rodney would have released whatever it was pent up in him and turned and come humbly back to the quiet quays and canals, had not the engine suddenly spluttered.

At once Rodney was delving expertly into it, poking, dipping, trying to spark it to life. Then he straightened up and looked at Sophie.

"Something wrong?" she asked.

"No."

"But it's stopped."

"Yes. No gas. We've run clear out of gas."

"Isn't that something wrong?"

"Not with the engine," defended Rodney jealously, jealous for the boat, "but with the hire firm. They told me I had enough for two hours."

"Two hours of quays and canals, perhaps. You would eat up more in open water. Oh, Rodney, what are we to do?"

The boy was looking around them. They had come right through the passage now and the coast looked a long way off.

"If we drifted further in I could swim to shore and fix up some gas to see us back."

"Is there a drift in that direction?"

"No," Rodney admitted.

"Then?"

Rodney said nothing.

They sat silent for a while. For a rather busy water-way there was no traffic at all. Of course, though, it was a weekday, and it was only on Saturdays and Sundays that the boating enthusiasts came out in their throngs.

"Rodney, we must do something," Sophie despaired. "We can't just sit here."

"If you can see an island with a fisherman's cottage I could swim there. I wouldn't like leaving you for the time it would take me to get to the mainland, but a nearer island would do."

"I wouldn't allow you to go to either of them. It would be too far."

"Swimming is like walking to me," he scorned. "But I don't like leaving you. You could drift into shallows if you didn't know what to look out for. You could strike rock."

"Can we paddle with our hands?" Sophie said desperately.

"It's a bit big for that," he shrugged.

"Yes. Why did you hire such a large boat?"

"I've always had boats this size," Rodney said rather sulkily, not answering her question.

"You were allowed down here to row, never to captain a yacht," went on Sophie positively.

"This isn't a yacht, it's a—"

"Well, whatever you call it!" Sophie said quite sharply. She narrowed her eyes to the passage again through which they had passed, and had now drifted away from, drifted almost a quarter of a mile she estimated. To her joy she saw a boat emerging from the broadwater.

"Rodney," she commanded excitedly, "wave!"

Rodney looked at the distant boat, but he did not move.

"Rodney!"

"We'll drift in, in time," he told Sophie. "I'm sure of it, the current here does a kind of circle, I've been watching it. Sophie . . . Miss Arthur, if you wave over that boat I'm going to feel all kinds of a fool."

"Nonsense, Rodney, lots of people run out of gas, it's no sin."

"I hate asking anyone for help."

"Well, you can hate as much as you like, *I* am asking for it." Sophie got up, waved a scarf, waved a towel, screamed at the top of her voice. She put everything into her effort, she never stopped her effort. In a few minutes she saw that her work had not been in vain. The boat, a mini fishing trawler, was

105

cutting across to them.

In all this time Rodney had not spoken. Even when the trawler came alongside he left the talking to Sophie. She explained their predicament and was rewarded with enough fuel to see them back again. Only as the trawler was leaving was anything said to Rodney.

"Next time, young feller," advised the skipper shortly, "do first things first. Check."

He left them, and Sophie said crossly to Rodney: "You could at least have said Yes to him, even if you couldn't bring yourself to say thank you."

"I was made to look a fool," suffered Rodney.

"Well, you were, weren't you?" said Sophie exasperated.

"Yes," Rodney admitted surprisingly, and he looked at Sophie with honest eyes—and as well as honesty *with something else*.

Sophie saw it and recognised it for what it was. The *un*-loving instead of the loving look. The boy did not love her any longer. There would be no more long gazes, no more flowers flung at windows. No one loves someone who has made them ridiculous, even though they deserved ridicule, it was all as simple . . . *and telling* . . . as that.

"Oh, Rodney," Sophie said a little sadly.

"You're obstructing my view, Miss Arthur, can you sit more to the portside," said Rodney.

When they had returned the boat to the hiring firm, Rodney refused Sophie's offer of a ride back to Apa-Kingsley.

"But how will you get there?"

"Mr. Bethel is down in the mini bus, there's a surf carnival and he's brought some of the Sixth to watch it."

"But you don't like organized things."

106

"I think I may try to like them."

"You do that, Rodney—and, dear—"

"Yes?"

"What happened today stays a secret. I think it's better that way."

"That's for you to say," was all Rodney returned.

As she drove home, Sophie thought a little resentfully that Rodney could at least have thanked her for her offer of silence. He could have been in a pack of trouble doing what he had . . . but then, with a bite of her lip, she could have, too. She had had no right to have conceded to him.

Well, all was well that ended well, and the episode had at least ended without mishap. Then, turning into the school gates, Sophie saw something that looked like a beginning, not an ending. In front of the entrance a taxi truck was drawn up, and many pieces of luggage were being carried in. A new pupil? No, pupils were strictly restricted to two bags apiece.

"It's Mrs. Saxby," called Marion Javes excitedly by Sophie's side the moment Sophie alighted. "Did you ever see such lovely suitcases? Pigskin every one of them!" She sighed.

"Has she arrived herself?"

"Oh, yes, and I can tell you she's pigskin, too, I mean by that she's quality, of course."

"Of course," said Sophie, and turning away she took the back steps up to Honor's flat.

She had known there was somebody, there had been that photo on his, Garrick Saxby's, table, but he had implied that he would not need the best suite yet, and Sophie had taken it that he had been awaiting a decision from his fiancée, *not his wife*. Not Mrs. Saxby. No, she had not thought that.

She looked around for Father, intending to tell him to pack his things. Though he was still bandaged up, he could move a little, and quite liked to. They must empty Honor's flat at once for the Chief and the Chief's wife.

Father was not around. Since the accident, once he was carried downstairs, he stopped there until he was finished for the day. Deciding not to waste time looking for him, Sophie began to bundle up her belongings, the same as she had once before. With only her nose and eyes showing above a pile of towels she tottered along the corridor to the minor suite . . . and into something large and human and male . . .

"Not again!" said an irritated voice. "Do you always have to do things twice, Miss Arthur?"

Sophie looked up at Garrick Saxby with anger. "If you'd told me Mrs. Saxby was coming so soon I would have gone ahead last time and got it all over and done with."

"How would I know?" he came back.

"Not know your w—" She felt the bottom towel slipping and grabbed at it. Grabbed too late. All the towels slipped across the corridor floor.

"Look," he said, helping her pick them up, kneeling beside her where she knelt, "stop playing the fool, won't you, and stay where you are."

"On the floor?"

"Stop it!" he said, and there was a note of warning in his voice she could not disobey.

"Stay in the school's best suite?" she corrected.

"Yes."

"But—"

"This present flat is quite ample."

"It's still not the best. The Head should always have the best." The headmaster's wife as well, Sophie added under her breath. Mrs. Headmaster.

"It has a stunning view," she reminded him weakly, feeling his eyes boring down on her, and wondering whether he had heard her under-her-breath sotto voice.

If he had, he did not comment. He said testily: "This apartment is quite adequate, Miss Arthur. Kindly leave it at that."

"But the view—"

"A view is the last thing in the world that would concern Mrs. Saxby. She is essentially a person for people, not sights and sounds."

"I like people, too," Sophie could not resist defending herself.

"Thank you for informing me. I hadn't noticed. No, Eve would not even look through the window. I assure you of that." A tolerant smile. "My Eve has other ideas."

"Flowers?" Why was she probing like this? Why was she so anxious to know? Eve. Such a lovely name. Not like Sophie. Not wisdom.

"I told you she liked people. Yet flowers it is, too, in a way, for what else are children than flowers in the garden of life?"

"How very nice," Sophie said spontaneously, but at once he dampened her with his:

"Oh, yes, I can be nice, Miss Arthur."

"I never said you couldn't."

"It's amazing how near you can get to saying something without saying it. You seem to have that talent. You should have been given a drama class, not a nature study."

"They speak their lines in drama," Sophie proffered.

"Yet subtly imply as well. But back to the flowers of life."

"Children?"

"Yes. Eve has an intense feeling for the young. Put the snubbiest, grubbiest small child and the Niagara

Falls in front of her, and she wouldn't even be aware of the spectacle of water."

"Even when she bathed the grubby child?" grinned Sophie.

"It would be a labour of love."

"Then why don't you—" Sophie stopped herself in time. You could scarcely say to your Head: "Then why don't you and your wife have a family?"

"Take these things back, Miss Arthur," Garrick Saxby ordered, "take them at once."

"I don't like doing it. After all, you are the principal."

"As principal I'm telling you to go back to the suite you have now."

"Yes, sir," Sophie said.

"Then after you've deposited them, return here immediately to take tea with Eve and with me."

"But—"

"Your father is already in the flat and getting along famously with Mrs. Saxby."

"Father always gets on with people."

"Especially when the topic is babies," Garrick Saxby insinuated.

"Babies?"

"You, as one." He gave a hateful smile. "Now hurry along, or the conversation will leave all the little endearing things you used to do, like gurgling, like waving your chubby fist, and start on your childish complaints. Not nearly so pleasant. If you come back in time you can steer the conversation away from measles and mumps to something less embarrassing." Again the hateful grin. "Skidoo," he said, and clapped his hands.

Sophie would dearly have loved not to have returned at all, but she knew by now that when Garrick Saxby issued an order, it was just that, an order. Anyway, she did not want him to hear how many spots she had had, how her face had puffed up.—Also she was curious about Eve Saxby. "Pigskin," Marion Javes had described, "real quality."

But when Sophie tapped on the flat door and was told to enter she knew that for once Marion had been *under*stating. Eve Saxby was quality all right, but she was also the loveliest woman Sophie had ever seen. Sophie stood just gazing at Eve's tall grace, at her coppery hair, her violet eyes and faintly carnation-washed skin, and knew life to be totally unfair.

"Yes," said Garrick Saxby, who had come to let Sophie in, "it is unjust, isn't it, Miss Arthur, but if it's any consolation to you you're not the first one to cry to heaven for vengeance."

"Cry to—"

"We can't all be beautiful," and he gave that hateful tilted grin of his again. He put his fingers under Sophie's arm and led her into the room and announced:

"Eve dear, this is Sophia Arthur, once the chubby baby Mr. Arthur has been describing so paternally, and Miss Arthur, this is the one and only Eve Saxby."

CHAPTER SIX

It was not the usual introduction, but then Garrick Saxby was not a usual person. With beauty such as Eve's, Sophie decided, neither could his wife be.

Sophie watched covertly as Eve poured tea and milked and sugared it to Sophie's liking. Hands like white moths fluttering over cups, she recalled from her novelette teens, and she half-glanced to her own brown paws, short and square of nail, a little blunt in shape and in obvious need of creaming.

She looked up again to find Garrick Saxby's amused eyes on her—and on her hands. He wore a wry half smile and she knew he had guessed her thoughts. All this and white moths as well, his eyes telegraphed teasingly, and Sophie writhed.

But she still could not help herself from warming to Eve, the older girl was one of those people you like, and feel you could even get to love, at once.

Eve left Mr. Arthur's side to come and sit by Sophie.

"You and I are to be friends," she said charmingly. "Garrick has said so."

"I'm sure we will," returned Sophie, "even without his bidding."

Eve looked slightly surprised at that. "He didn't intend to be authoritative," she assured her . . . (I bet he did, Sophie thought) . . . "he just worked it out that as we're the two younger ones in the school, that is among the adults, if you follow me, Sophie—"

"I follow you."

"That naturally we shall seek each other's company."

"I'm sure of it. But he's wrong. The Headmaster is quite wrong, there's *three* of us, not two. The third is the boys' phys edder, name of Bill Bethel."

"Is he—"

"About our vintage? Yes." Without turning to check up, Sophie had a distinct impression of disapproving tightness from the direction of Garrick Saxby. She decided to catch him out, and did turn. She was right, the Headmaster looked very displeased with her.

"Isn't that correct, sir?" she asked blandly.

"Oh, Bethel? Yes, I guess so."

"But you didn't tell me, Garrick," reproached Eve, "you never mentioned anyone else."

Garrick Saxby shrugged and handed Eve his cup for a refill. When she had poured it for him, he turned his attention to Mr. Arthur, but still listening, Sophie could tell, to any further exchange between the two girls.

He need not have worried. The conversation was completely innocuous.

"Tell me about the school," begged Eve. She paused. "Particularly about the little ones."

"Not so little, Mrs. Saxby."

"Eve, Sophie."

"Not so little, Eve. You see, we don't take any tiny tots here, we actually only start at the junior school, there's neither a pre-prep nor a kindergarten."

"But that's a shame. Garrick" . . . turning to the Headmaster . . . "you simply must incorporate a kindergarten."

"That would call for another teacher, Eve."

"I could do it," Eve offered eagerly.

"Headmaster," came in Sophie smoothly, "doesn't

care about unqualified instructors." She pretended deep interest in the cream filling of the biscuit she had selected.

"That's true," said Garrick Saxby calmly. "To run a good school you must have good teachers."

"Good *qualified* teachers," inserted Sophie, still smoothly. She bit into the biscuit.

"Naturally," he agreed. "What else?"

"I believe you could be quite good yet not have passed an exam," broke in Eve.

"If all this is an attempt to overflow an already sufficiently filled school with little pattering feet, it's a waste of time," said Garrick. "The answer is *no*." He turned definitely to Mr. Arthur again.

Eve was smiling ruefully at Sophie. "Garrick was always like that," she sighed, "he always knew what he wanted and saw to it that he got it."—The Head, noted Sophie, was listening-in again. She also noted that although Eve complained about Garrick Saxby, it was only a gentle, affectionate complaint. Well, that was how, with married partners, it should be.

"Don't worry, Eve," she reassured her, "there are lots of small ones who will need you."

"*I* need them," Eve confided. "Am I silly?"

"Just very nice." Sophie impulsively touched her hand and received a responsive press in reply.

Sophie finished her tea and got up. "Coming, Father?" she asked.

Garrick Saxby had risen too. "Stay as you are, Mr. Arthur, I'll get a couple of the seniors to give you a hand . . . or should it be a foot? . . . back to the front suite." A fatuous smile.

"I'm quite capable, Headmaster," Mr. Arthur assured him.

"You have a broken kneecap." It sounded almost like a reminder, Sophie thought, and her father . . .

reminded? . . . agreed at once.

"Yes," he said, and sat back to talk to Eve once more until Morris, or Phelps, or any of the larger senior boys could come and get him along to Honor's apartment.

Sophie saw that Garrick Saxby was holding the door open for her, so she went across.

He did not speak all the way down the passage, and at the end of the passage where he should have descended the stairs he carried on with Sophie. When she paused at the door of the best suite, waiting for him to leave her, he leaned deliberately over her and turned the doorhandle. When she did not enter the room before him, he calmly went in first. Sophie, fuming, followed.

He used no preamble.

"Miss Arthur, there was no call to have made a threesome out of a twosome just now."

"What do you mean?"

"I mean you two girls being around the same age I thought it would be a good thing for you and Eve to be together, but I did not include Bill Bethel."

"What have you against Mr. Bethel?"

"Nothing, most certainly nothing."

"Then—"

"Look, my idea was a kind of girls together, something that Eve has enjoyed little of, if at all, and not—well—"

"Not male and female, created He them," came in Sophie promptly.

"Exactly."

"But you couldn't expect to keep her away from him, from any of the men, indefinitely." What a monster of a husband, Sophie thought.

"Not so much from men as a whole, but certainly from one man in particular."

"You mean Bill?"

"As around her own age, yes."

"Mr. Saxby, this is all quite ridiculous! You can't shut her up, you can't cloister her."

"I can't, and I wouldn't, but I certainly don't intend to spread her around."

"I just don't understand." Sophie did, all right, but she could scarcely say: "I can't follow such absolute possessiveness, such suspicion, such jealousy, such blind stubborn determination."

He came in coldly: "There is no need for you to understand, only a need for you to be with Eve, perhaps be with Eve and Bethel, but not to encourage Eve and Bethel to be together *without you*. Now do you follow me?"

"I follow you, but——"

"Then that's all that's needed," he cut in. "I'll be watching you, Miss Arthur."

"Not watching your—not watching Eve?"

"I know my Eve," he said shortly. "I know she'll like Bill Bethel at once, as she would like any good-looking young man who happened to be around."

"Perhaps," said Sophie, a little nettled, "*he* won't like her."

"My dear Miss Arthur!"

The cold patronage in his voice antagonized Sophie. "It could be," she persisted. "Not everyone has similar tastes. Besides——"

"Besides?"

"Besides, Bill . . . Mr. Bethel . . . has made it very clear that——"

"Yes?"

"That he could be interested in me." Sophie tilted her chin. Damn him, she thought, the way he over-rides me you'd think I was less than the dust!

"Of course," agreed the Headmaster, "you were the

only eligible female at the time. Also, you are not at all . . . well . . ."

"Yes?"

"It doesn't matter," he shrugged. "But what does matter is Eve and Bethel. I am always a believer in prevention, Miss Arthur, so if a few pertinent words now can prevent a situation later I won't shrink from them."

"Do please tell me the preventive words."

"Gladly. You said just now that Bill Bethel was interested in you?"

"I said I thought he could be."

"Yes, and I quite agree with that, but it still doesn't cancel out the wisdom of precautions."

"Precautions?" she queried.

"Against Bethel."

"But I just told you—"

"Yes, you told me, but" . . . cruelly . . . "how could our young gymnast ever look your way when there was Eve's way? How, Miss Arthur?"

"You're abominable!" spluttered Sophie.

"But factual?"

"You're speaking only for yourself."

"As it happens that's what I'm *not* doing," he said cryptically, or cryptic it seemed to Sophie. "But I naturally can't vouch for Bethel."

"You're abominable?" she repeated. "You're not only dictatorial, belligerent, cold as ice, unsympathetic, bossy, impossible, you—you're an obnoxious pig as well. All right then, perhaps I am as ugly as sin, but let me tell you, Headmaster, that if I were your Eve—"

She did not finish. Making sure that the door was closed, that no one saw them, he took and shook her . . . and shook her . . . deliberately shook her.

"I never said that, Sophie, I never thought that.

My God, girl, you must know you're a flower."

"Cauli variety." She pulled away angrily.

He let her go, but he stood watching her narrowly

"No wonder," he said, "at the age of—what is i again?"

"It doesn't matter."

"No wonder at that age you're still *Miss* Arthur. No wonder, since you haven't the art of accepting com pliments in a complimentary manner. I happen to have meant that."

"Thank you, sir," Sophie said ungraciously. "So can I go now?"

"No. This happens to be your apartment, so I wil go. But please not to forget what I've said."

"Which part?" Impudently.

"Eve, of course."

"As her contemporary in age and so presumably in outlook I'm to divert Mrs. Saxby, be a companion to her, but never permit Bill Bethel to do likewise."

"You catch on," he awarded.

"But I don't comprehend," Sophie said, "I comprehend jealousy, and commend it in a kind of way between two close people, but possessiveness, no."

"Possessiveness?"

"You would like to shut Eve away, wouldn't you?"

"As a matter of fact, yes."

"And you call that love?"

"Love?" He looked at her in complete bewilderment. "Where does love come into it?"

"It generally sneaks in somewhere in such instances, shows between the chinks, however meagrely, in most marriages."

"What marriage?"

She stared back at him. "Why, why—yours."

"With whom?"

"With Eve."

A minute went by in silence, then :

"What in tarnation gave you that idea?"

"*Mrs*. Saxby." But Sophie said it faintly. Her heart was thudding all at once, thudding madly, expectantly, she felt sure he must hear it.

"Mrs. Terry Saxby," Garrick Saxby said harshly. "Eve is the widow of my cousin Terence Saxby. I never dreamed you didn't know."

"How would I know?" Sophie paused. "How would I even be interested enough to want to know?"

He nodded coolly, accepting that. "I suppose, too, such a mistake could be made—the same name, etcetera, etcetera. However, I still think you should have reached a different conclusion."

"How do you mean, Headmaster?"

"Do you think I would have taken my *wife* into less than the best suite?"

"You said Eve didn't bother about views. That's why we agreed not to move."

"But my *wife* would care about moons coming up out of the Pacific, my *wife* would care about stars caught on top of a penthouse. If she didn't, then by God she would soon be taught."

"By whom? Like me, you're not a qualified teacher, remember." Sophie withdrew a pace, a little scared at his thunderous look.

For a moment she thought he was going to shake her again, or—do something, for he actually stepped across. Then he paused, turned round, left.

Sophie still stood where she had retreated. So Eve Saxby was *not* Mrs. Garrick Saxby, *not* the Headmaster's wife. Then why was she here? Admittedly she was a young widow, but most young widows were capable of looking after themselves. Why had Garrick Saxby given so many instructions about Eve? Why was Bill Bethel taboo?

Then it came to Sophie in a flash, came clearly and undeniably. Men did not safeguard their cousin's . . cousin's, mark you, not even brother's . . . widow unless—unless—

He loves her, Sophie knew. For all his denial Garrick Saxby loves the lovely Eve. Probably it was too early yet for him to speak. Perhaps his cousin was not long dead. But Garrick wants her, and, as Eve herself said, what that man wants, he gets. He feels he must not let Eve out of his sight, so he has brought her here to Apa, and since naturally he can't be with her all the time, *I* am to take over in his absence. I am to help make what is to be, be. I am the ordered accomplice. But what, Mr. Saxby, if instead—

She said the last to herself, standing by the window as she looked down at Bill Bethel coming back from a game of tennis. How lean and brown and young and attractive he was, Sophie suddenly thought . . . and she wondered wickedly if Eve would have the same thoughts.

Most of all she wondered if she dared to find out. . . .

Eve was an immediate success with all the school. Copper hair and violet eyes would have to be, Sophie knew, but she knew, too, had Eve been a flower, cauli variety, as Garrick Saxby had *not* corrected when Sophie had said it, she would still have been popular.

She was friendly to everybody, almost pathetically eager for their friendship in return. It was, puzzled Sophie on more than one occasion, as though the girl had been starved of affection.

All the other teachers, both male and female, liked her—no generation gap there, all the pupils, from the susceptible senior classes to the smallest firstgrader. The boys openly drooled over her, the girls saw in Eve what they would like to become themselves. The littlies came to her as a favourite aunt.—"No, not as a mother," Eve sighed sadly, "not as I *want*."

"Darling" . . . Sophie and Eve were at that stage by now . . . "you'll have oodles of your own babies."

"One would do to begin with."

"Were you always like this, Eve? Mother-slanted, I mean?"

"Always. I was born a pram peeper, see a baby carriage and I had to find out what was in it. Were you like that?"

"No," admitted Sophie. She could have felt jealous of Eve's success with the children had she not known that although they adored Eve, Sophie was the one who was one of them. The same mistakes, the same ups and downs, the same awkwardnesses. But still it would be nice to be gracious like Eve, Sophie yearned.

In all this examination and conclusion, she had not yet dealt with Bill Bethel. But she soon found she had no need to. For as soon as Bill had met Eve, Sophie knew that what she had asked herself could she dare try out, and that was to disobey Garrick Saxby and let the two young people come together, that the matter was out of her hands. For Bill looked at Eve as though he disbelieved what he saw. Headmaster was right, Sophie knew ruefully, who would look at a flower (cauli) when there was a lovely orchid like Eve?

Eve in her turn liked Bill at once. It could be that he was the only younger male in the staff, but several times Sophie surprised a meeting of two pairs of eyes, violet, bright blue (Bill's) and knew it was not as simple as that.

When one of the girls came running over one afternoon to tell Sophie that Headmaster wished Miss Arthur to come to the office, Sophie felt sure it would be about Eve and Bill. The "keeper", as Garrick

Saxby had made her, had not been "keeping" properly, those two, Eve and Bill, had been seen too much together. Sophie thought this wryly as she crossed the quadrangle and went into the office.

The Headmaster was not sitting at his desk but standing by the window when she tapped quietly and entered. He did not turn until she gave a little indicating cough.

"Miss Arthur," he acknowledged. "Please sit down." He sat on the other side of the table.

"It's Mrs. Saxby and Mr. Bethel, isn't it?" said Sophie before he could, thinking it would help her to beat him to the post. "Well, I could scarcely stand between them, they're neither of them children to be told what to do."

"Go on," he encouraged.

"I can't help them finding each other easy to talk to, I—I can't drag Eve away by the hair."

"Proceed, please."

"Then Bill Bethel . . . well, it was all just as you said it would be. One look at Eve and he—well—"

"He had no eyes for the other flower." Garrick cocked his ear towards Sophie. "Don't I hear you inserting 'cauli variety'?"

"If this is all a joke, as you seem to be making it now, you should have told me so at first, not put me into an invidious position."

"Miss Arthur?"

"You did. You made a watchdog of me."

"If I did such a thing, and I rather thought my request was 'girls together', you've proved a very poor Fido."

"Watchdogs are not called Fido," said Sophie foolishly, something in this man always brought out the child in her somehow, "they're Caesar, or Chieftain, or—"

"Enough," he came in curtly. "Enough of this topic as well. I didn't send for you, Miss Arthur, to criticize your failure with Eve and Bill Bethel—"

"Failure?" she queried.

He held up an authoritative hand. "I brought you here in the hope that you might be able to explain this." He passed across a sheet of paper, and she looked at it. It was, she saw, an account.

The last thing that would have occurred to Sophie was that this could be a genuine request for assistance from this man. Everything that Garrick Saxby did had an undertone for her, another side to it. She looked at the account again, though not, in the heat of her resentment, very accurately, and saw from the letterhead that it came from a maritime firm.

"Of all the unfriendly gestures," she burst out in indignation, jumping at once to an incorrect conclusion, "and they talk about lending a helping hand! If they'd meant to charge for it, why didn't they say so at once? We only took a cup or so of petrol, no more." Her voice stopped abruptly, stopped as she realized . . . too late . . . she was saying too much. She knew it by Saxby's sudden alert expression.

"We, Miss Arthur?"

"Rodney. Me."

"Rodney . . . oh, yes, the Fini Island boy. But how do you fit in?" He had put his elbows on the desk, his chin in his palms, and he was staring directly at her. "Where are you included, Miss Arthur?"

There was not the remotest hope of escaping, Sophie thought dismally. If ever she felt like kicking herself, she felt like it now. If she had only probed around first . . . held her tongue . . .

"You told Rodney to exercise," she said inadequately.

"I recall that. Bethel had reported to me that the

123

boy didn't seem to take to team occupations, so I suggested he get behind a pair of blades."

"Yes," Sophie said faintly.

"But he didn't, did he?" A glance at the account.

"I think he gave it some thought," Sophie defended, "and I know he will certainly do it if he goes down to the coast again, but—"

"But?"

"Rodney worked it out that it might be better to get to know the quay and canals first—they can be tricky, you know."

"Keep on."

"So he thought he would do such a thing quicker and more accurately with power."

"Hands are power."

"I meant engine power," Sophie said wretchedly.

"Whereupon you praised such resourcefulness?"

"Oh, no, I didn't, I didn't know anything about it until I got there."

"You?"

"Yes."

"You actually had a rendezvous with the lad?"

"Oh, don't be silly, it was nothing like that."

"But you met him?" he insisted.

"I went down to the river. To the old Kingsley boathouse."

"Whence Rodney had brought his hired power boat from this firm" . . . he tapped the account . . . "to pick you up?"

"From that firm? You mean the account is not from—"

"Just go on, Miss Arthur, please. You saw Rodney in a power boat and you clapped your hands and jumped aboard?"

"Oh, no. I implicitly told Rodney that I didn't think that this was the kind of exercise you had in mind."

"That," he said, "would be the understatement of the year. But please go on."

"Rodney said what he did about getting to know the river design first, and I could see the sense."

"With a river jaunt awaiting you I can well believe that. But go on."

"There's not much more," Sophie tried to evade, but with a certain feeling that she had gone past evasion, "we did just that—explored. Rodney said" . . . eagerly . . . "that there's more exercise than people think at the back of a wheel."

"No doubt," the Headmaster came in, "he said that. But carry on."

"I told you" . . . a little wildly . . . "that was all."

"Then why this account? Why your indignant complaint about helping hands that ask for payment for their help?"

"That was a mistake. I mean, I jumped to a wrong conclusion."

"You've been doing a lot of wrong jumping, Miss Arthur. But go on."

"We ran out of petrol."

"No disaster, surely? None of the quays, or canals, nor the river itself, are that wide. Either the boy . . . or you, for that matter, for I seem to recall that you can swim . . . could have got ashore and solved the problem. Even pulled into a marina, or moored at a jetty."

"We weren't in a quay or canal."

"Nor, I am beginning to suspect, on the river."

"No, sir."

"Then where in damnation were you, Miss Arthur? Not in the broadwater?"

"No."

"Not—farther than that?"

"Yes."

"The sea?"

There was a pause, then : "Yes," admitted Sophie.

"My God!" Garrick Saxby exclaimed.

She did not look at his face, but she could see his tightly clasped hands, the knuckle bones showing white on the brown skin. Anger, she thought abstractedly.

"So you floated around for a while." His voice was deceptively calm.

"Yes. Rodney wanted to swim ashore, but I wouldn't let him."

"Noble," Saxby nodded, but he did not explain whether it was noble of Rodney or noble of Sophie.

"We were wondering what we could do when we saw this small trawler coming through Tippler's Passage. I waved and screamed—"

"Not Rodney?"

"Rodney was humiliated. They saw us, came across and helped us out. That" . . . defiantly . . . "was all, Headmaster."

"Thank you," he said, "thank you for telling me something I would have known nothing about" . . . a pause . . . "*had you not informed me.*"

The emphasis was unmistakable. She had jumped too quickly to a wrong conclusion, she knew. She looked miserably at him. "You mean—"

"I mean this account has nothing at all to do with that, your good Samaritans were genuinely good, they gave and forgot. No, Miss Arthur, this bill is a different cup of tea. Kindly read it once more."

Sophie did, and saw what she would have seen had she not, in her guilt, rushed her fences. The account was addressed to Rodney (care of the school, so he must have given this address, the foolish boy) for returning the boat at a later hour than agreed. She recalled them coming back and depositing the boat, both eager to be done with a less-than-pleasant situation. If Rodney had seen the proprietor and been told he owed extra money, no doubt he could have settled up immediately. If he hadn't, then Sophie would have. She was not aware that she was murmuring this aloud.

"So," said Garrick Saxby. He tapped the tips of his fingers together. "You've been quite friendly with Rodney?" he asked.

"He needed friendship. He's a late starter, so in a way just as confused as our first-graders."

"But surely your help could have taken the form of a word of advice now and then, a cheerful conversation, the loan perhaps of a book."

"How little," broke in Sophie, "do you understand!"

"What, Miss Arthur?"

"He was lost. *Lost*. He had to be found."

"And you did that sitting pretty on a launch?"

"I'm not pretty, and as it happens I didn't. I only solved one thing, and it wasn't that."

"What was it, Miss Arthur?"

What more could she hide? Sophie thought wearily; this man had the knack of uncovering everything.

"Rodney foolishly believed he liked me," she submitted.

"Very foolish."

"The incident killed it. No man, no boy, cares any more about someone who has made them seem a fool."

"In other words you're troubled by calf love no longer?"

"No, Mr. Saxby."

"And Rodney, is he troubled?"

"Only unless you trouble him over this incident."

She looked down at the account.

"You actually think I should pass it over?"

"Yes. You see, it's all going to be different now. I think Rodney is going to begin to mix."

"He hasn't made a bad fist of mixing even without trying," Garrick Saxby said drily.

"I mean with youngsters his own age, not with seniors like me. I think if you ask Bill Bethel . . ." Sophie could have bitten her tongue, could have swallowed back that 'Bill Bethel'. "I think you'll learn," she said, "that Rodney already is joining a team or so." She looked brightly at Saxby, hoping he had not been reminded of anything by her mention of the sports master's name, but it was a forlorn hope.

"Ah, yes, Mr. Bethel," Garrick Saxby said. "So we come to another subject. He and my cousin-in-law appear to be seeing a great deal of each other."

Sophie did not answer. What she felt like retorting was :

"What if he has, Mr. Saxby . . . unless it's that you have plans other than cousin-in-law for Eve, is that it?"

But she just sat.

"I know I can't put her in a tower, tie her up, as you once told me, but I do believe, Miss Arthur, that it's very important that there is no entanglement for Eve. Not yet."

Still Sophie said nothing.

"You've done your best, I suppose, just as you did with Rodney. But it seems you're not the kind that gets results." He sighed.

Angered by his sigh, Sophie said : "There's always a solution if you're dissatisfied. You can always dismiss me."

"I can't do that. Not yet."

"You sound as though you intend to do it some

time."

"Oh, I certainly do," he assured her.

She sat on uncomfortably for a few moments, then asked quietly if there was anything else.

"No. You can go. Oh, you can send Rodney in."

"You're not going to—"

"No, Miss Arthur, I'm not. I'm going to say Good boy. Can you show me how to handle an inboard? No, of course, Rodney, you don't need to settle this account, the school will gladly do it.

"Well, phys ed mistress" . . . as Sophie still stood there . . . "what are you waiting for now?"

"Nothing," Sophie blurted, and fled.

She had no classes, she was not on duty, so she walked across to the garden. About to push the little picket gate to the fence that had been built around the flower beds to keep them sacrosanct from the hurly-burly of vigorous school life, Sophie paused. There were two figures under the arch of an allamander. Eve was reaching up for one of the allamander's fabullous yellow flowers, but Bill Bethel was saving her the arduous stretch by doing the plucking himself. But when he had finished, he did not hand the lovely blossom to Eve, he leaned down and tucked it in her hair. The soft yellow petals against the burnt copper curls made Sophie catch her breath. She wondered if Bill had put the flower above the correct ear, for though Eve was widowed and so presumably eligible again, wasn't she already promised? Sophie bit her lip. Now, according to Headmaster Saxby, was the time when she should step forward and break up the little scene, be the "keeper" he had appointed her. What if she obeyed him and called: "Eve, don't you remember telling me that what Garrick Saxby wants, he gets? Bill—"

But what Sophie would have said to Bill was never resolved, for the two, Eve and Bill, turned away at that moment and began walking to the hibiscus corner, and though that was all there was to it, a walk together, Sophie saw their hands brushing . . . and felt tears in her eyes. She stepped back.

The tears were still there as she crossed the quadrangle, so that she did not see Father until she was almost upon him. Mr. Arthur had not seen her, either.

"I suppose you're wondering what the old man is doing without his bodyguard," he said to Sophie. "Well, the knee felt so good I decided I'd try it out."

"Of course, darling." Through her tear-obscured eyes Sophie blinked at her father and thought that though his knee felt good, he certainly didn't look good. But undoubtedly she wasn't seeing clearly. Those young lovers had torn at her. Suddenly she had felt outside of everything. A kind of—not wanted. Father wanted her, of course, but—

"Darling," she said suddenly and unexpectedly, unexpectedly even to herself: "Father darling, you're not going to do anything final like leaving me?"

He did not speak for a while.

"It comes, Sophie," he reminded her gently. Again he paused. "Shall we talk about it?"

"Oh, no, no!" She caught his arm urgently, and with the softest of sighs he complied.

She left him at the verandah, for emerging from the headmaster's office she could see Rodney Berthold.

She intercepted him a little nervously.

"Rodney . . ."

"Oh, Miss Arthur." Rodney sounded very cheerful and extremely well adjusted.

"You've been having a session with the Head."

"No, it was a chat," Rodney assured her happily. "He's a great cove, understands perfectly. He was rather in the same boat himself when he was young . . . I say, that's a pun, in the same boat."

"Yes," said Sophie, unable to raise a smile.

"No boat, though, he came from the far west, had correspondence education the same as I had, until the dread day when he had to mix. He knows exactly how I felt."—*Felt*, noted Sophie, not feel any more.

"Was it awful, Rodney?"

"Rotten."

"I'm sorry, it was my fault, I didn't mean to give you away."

"Oh, you mean in the Head's office? No, it was great. I thought you meant trying to settle down. That was awful. But it's all over now."

"Were you pulled up about the hiring?"

"No, only had to pay up. Pretty decent of him, really, because I was playing the fool."

"Good boy," murmured Sophie. "Can you show me how to handle an inboard? No, you needn't settle this account, the school will do it."

"I just told you I paid up," Rodney reminded her, "but he did say part of the other things." He stared at her. "How did you know?"

"Just put it down to intuition," suggested Sophie. She turned away.

Rodney turned, too. But he turned again after a few steps.

"He really is some guy," he said admiringly. "I told him—well, about us."

"Us?"

"I mean me. How I'd *thought* I felt about you, Miss Arthur, and how I suddenly could laugh instead. He said it is like that, and to appreciate it, because very soon you don't laugh any more."

"No," said Sophie, "you're serious instead, you know what you want, and you get it."—But would

Garrick Saxby get what he wanted this time? He was strong, but was he as strong as two hands brushing casually as two people walked together? Except that he was Garrick Saxby, Sophie almost could have found it in her to feel sorry for him . . . except that any sorrow she had at this moment was strictly for Sophie Arthur herself.

CHAPTER SEVEN

Sophie could not have explained the deep unhappiness somewhere inside her in the days that followed. There was nothing to cause it. If ever life had revolved equably it was revolving that way now. There were no hitches, nothing to disturb or worry her. The episode of Rodney had concluded amiably, and Father of late was looking fairly well, she considered; most certainly he seemed very content.

Then why wasn't his daughter the same?

There had been no more stormy scenes with the headmaster, she had no school troubles, and every one of her swimming pupils could now swim. They would be ready to plunge in the school pool when it was officially opened in several weeks' time. In the meantime Sophie was continuing her classes down at the Isle of Capri Saxby house. She had become friendly with Mrs. Clayton, the housekeeper, who had told her that Mr. Saxby had owned the house for some years now and was holding it for some future . . . a knowing smile . . . occasion.

"I suppose he thinks he should bring his bride to a home, not a school," she had told Sophie. "And he will be bringing one, he practically said so. He said: 'I hope you'll still be available when Mrs. Saxby comes, for it's a big house.' He did not say when, but he was quite sure about Mrs. Saxby." A little indulgent laugh.

Of course he was sure, Sophie thought, when what

he wanted, he saw he got . . . but were Eve and Bill of the same mind?

There was nothing apparent between them, never any long conversations, never any escaping away together, but Sophie, and all the staff, ran down to the near-completed pool, one early morning, to try it out while its future occupants still slept, and skipping over the crisp, dew-wet grass, the morning smell of wild mountain lime sweet-acid in the air, Sophie saw Bill shortening his long steps to Eve's smaller ones. Again, unplanned yet somehow instinctive, their hands brushed, and Sophie felt her own hands incurling in sympathy . . . and in something else. Jealousy, she recognised, not jealousy for Bill, but jealousy for what that pair have between them. For she felt sure of it now.

"Not going in?" Garrick Saxby called across the pool to Sophie, and she dived at once, but for all her speed, he beat her to it. When she surfaced she was barely an inch away from him.

"Good morning, Miss Headmistress."

"Don't give me that ridiculous name!" she snapped.

"Well, you never made Miss Headmaster, did you?"

"If you mean my father didn't make it, why don't you say so?" She tured to begin swimming to the other end, but he swam underwater and rose in front of her again.

"Good morning, Miss Arthur."

She did not answer.

"If you don't reply, I'll do what I did down on the surfing beach, hold you under."

She knew now that what he said, he meant.

"Good morning, Headmaster," she conceded, and this time she escaped.

But that was the only ripple in a very calm pond

for Sophie. Other . . . qualified . . . members of the staff had ripples, but as Sophie had nothing to do with the scholastic side of Apa-Kingsley, she was not over-concerned . . . even over Virginia. For from evidence from Miss Prentice, several others of the teachers, Virginia Pederson, their shining hope for the forthcoming state exam, was not forthcoming any longer.

"Over-study," diagnosed Miss Prentice. "I've seen it happen time after time. She was at her peak a month ago, but the exam isn't for another month yet. I think she's gone stale."

"Her essays have," said May Perriman. "Where she sparkled previously, now she lags."

"Her parents will be desolated. Virginia is the third Pederson here, all bright and all achieving good results. But she doesn't seem keen any longer. Why?"

"Health O.K., Matron?" Garrick Saxby was there as well.

Matron said Yes.

"Taking her due of exercise, Miss Arthur?"

"Yes," Sophie reported.

"Then it must be staleness." He sighed. "A pity, it's a difficult thing to overcome. In fact the only way to defeat it is to put book right away for a while. But how do you do that in a school?"

"Virginia of all girls!" came in the geology teacher. "She was a perfect student."

"Too perfect too long."

"Seventeen is a difficult age."

"Perhaps the change of system did it."

"Perhaps—"

"I think," put in Eve, who had come in quietly, unnoticed, "she could be in love. Oh, yes" . . . at the startled looks . . . "Seventeen can fall in love."

"All ages fall in love, Evie," said Garrick Saxby humorously. "You should know that. What about you other ladies? Is that what ails our Virginia? Has she been bitten by the love bug?"

"I've never seen her even glance at the senior boys," they all reported.

"Then she must be in love with Galahad. She's taking King Arthur and the Round Table for her English, isn't she? I've seen it happen with boys, one even mooned over the Lady of Shalott for weeks. Perhaps it's Galahad and his strength of ten." Garrick Saxby laughed easily, they all laughed, and the subject of Virginia was shelved.

During the day Sophie was asked to go to the office.

She was thinking of Virginia as she crossed the quadrangle, wondering if this junior member of the staff, herself, Sophie Arthur, being nearer Virginia's age, was about to be asked to keep an eye on the girl . . . as she had been asked with Eve.

But it was not about Virginia that Garrick Saxby wished to speak.

"Have you had any experience of school bursary holders, Miss Arthur?" he began.

"Only after they've arrived here and I have them in my class," Sophie answered, puzzled that he should ask her. "Apa used to set an exam, and Honor selected the successful applicants, and that's all I know."

"Then you're to know more. You're to come up to a cane town called Sugar Hills."

"Yes, I've heard of it."

"And help me choose," he concluded.

She stared at him.

"But how can I choose, or help choose? I'm not certificated myself."

"That's why you're coming, I can't spare a teacher."

"I see," Sophie said, deflated. Presently she added: "Sugar Hills is more than a day's jaunt away."

"It's not a jaunt," he reminded her, "it's an elimination journey. We have room for two children only and there's a choice of five. They're all equally promising, the headmaster of the local state school has written. We'll have the task of selecting two of them."

"Are there any specific age vacancies? If there were you could choose the appropriate years, send for the qualifying pair, thus save yourself a journey."

"Also save you and Eve."

"Oh—Eve is coming!" Sophie was relieved about that.

"As you remarked, it's not merely a day's jaunt to Sugar Hills, we would need to stop, so we would need three people." His eyes flicked at Sophie. "I thought we could be spared several days."

"Yes," Sophie said.

"Then arrange for your lessons to be taken over by someone else and be ready to leave tomorrow morning."

"Yes, Headmaster," Sophie agreed. "Early?"

"Early," he concurred.

It was not even piccaninny daylight when Sophie awakened at a tap on her bedroom door. Still more asleep than awake, she ran across to open up, thinking it would be Father. It was only when Garrick Saxby handed her a cup of coffee and said: "Fifteen minutes" that Sophie became aware of her short, skimpy nightgown . . . the absence of a robe. That . . . and thank heaven, for there was no time now . . . she had packed last night along with the other things she would need. Certainly fifteen minutes would not have been sufficient time had she been unprepared.

She drank the coffee and scrambled into slacks and shirt. She went across to say goodbye to Father, but as he was still asleep she let it go. Seeing him asleep must have put her into a semi-daze herself again, for she climbed into the car beside Garrick Saxby and it was not until the Gold Coast was far behind them, the first approaches to Brisbane being made, that she realized that Eve was not there.

"Where's Eve?" she asked.

"She's not here."

"Yes, I can see that. Why?"

"She didn't care to come."

"And you accepted that?"

"Why not? Also, what is this, Miss Arthur? You're always telling me how I can't order her life, tie her up."

Sophie ignored that. "But you said she was coming," she protested.

"I did. She didn't."

"But—but it doesn't stop at that, does it?"

"It has stopped," he said finally. "She's there. We're here." He drove irritably for a few moments. "What do you want me to do? Turn back?"

"I don't want to go on."

"Then that is turn back, isn't it? We're doing no such thing."

"You lied to me!" she accused.

"I didn't. I said she would come, and she didn't come. It's as simple as that."

"It's not as simple. I don't believe you told her at all."

"Oh, yes, I did, but keeping in mind your criticism of my treatment of my cousin-in-law I made it more an invitation than an order. Well" . . . taking his eyes off the road for a moment . . . "isn't that what you would have advised?"

"You know I wouldn't . . . not when I myself was involved."

"Are you?"

"Am I what?"

"Involved."

She did not answer that, she could not trust herself to, so he kept on driving.

Presently they reached the northern capital, and though it was early he needed all his attention on the road and the traffic to break through to the Bruce Highway.

When at last they succeeded, he said: "I asked Eve if she would like—"

"If she would like—" burst in Sophie.

"To come. She politely declined. So—" A shrug.

"Mr. Saxby," said Sophie now, "*I* wouldn't have come had I known."

"Known what? That there was to be no third person, no chaperone? Good lord, woman, we're not going to the moon. We're going to a cane town called Sugar Hills to choose two out of five children. If you can concoct anything out of that then you should have been an English teacher dealing with the Romantic poets, not running on the double and touching your toes."

"I'm concocting nothing from it, only—"

"Only?"

"It's a long journey. Where" . . . a gulp . . . "do we stay tonight?"

"At a motel at adjourning Heathfell since Sugar Hills has nothing at all." A pause. "Two rooms." Another pause. "Not adjoining. Now if you don't mind, Miss Arthur, I've never seen this country before, and I've been assured that Buderim, and Nambour, and the beaches below them, and the Glasshouse Mountains to the west, comprise perhaps the loveliest terrain in the world."

She obeyed him . . . because she had seen it all before, and it was quite breathtakingly beautiful.

They began curving round the bases of the curious

mountains that once had won Captain Cook's interest. Fascinating fairybook peaks, around which you could imagine the Knights of the Round Table approaching in full gallop, mountains that rose to pinnacles, minarets, fingerpoints; no two alike. As the terrain reached up, the hills lost their green for a kind of floating blueness. It made for unreality, but the crops at their bases were very real . . . timber, fruit, nuts, and a plant that Sophie told Garrick was ginger. Here was the ginger jar of Australia. She pointed to the fields of sturdy green stalks with pushing scarlet shoots, and advised him to pause and take a long sniff.

"It's pungent," he said after he had done so, "I always thought ginger blossom was sweet and bridal."

"That's the white variety, Headmaster. This is not for a maiden's ear but for ginger in stoppered jars, in puddings, in beer, in bread."

"Gingerbread," he nodded, "the one that has gilt on it. Talking of guilt . . . with a *u* this time . . . are you still thinking in the same strain as you did before?"

"There," Sophie ignored, pointing to a patch between the clearing of trees, "is the coast. The Sunshine Coast." He looked briefly to where the terracotta earth stopped abruptly and a steep wooded descent took over, and caught . . . quite audibly caught . . . his breath. Sophie knew why.

It was an amazing scene. Far below them shimmered the Pacific Ocean, a sudden unfolding of shouting blue. But there were islands, too, the lilac islands of the southerly Barrier Reef group. It made for so much beauty you felt you could not keep pace with it.

"Yes, I know what you mean," Garrick said, and Sophie realized she had babbled her thoughts aloud.

They were silent almost into Nambour, except for Sophie's indication that the sky-high, or so it seemed, pineapple that rose out of the tropical orchards was not illusion, but a tourist pineapple.

"You can walk inside it," she said, "or if you like take a cane tram through the different tropical crops."

"Why is a cane train called a tram?"

"I don't know, but in Nambour the tram chunts right down the main street. I love cane country, do you?"

"I don't know." He said it sharply, and she wondered why.

"But you will," she assured him. "Cane in the wind is one of the loveliest things in the world."

Sophie barely had said it than the cane began, the cane that would extend for the rest of their journey to Sugar Hills, cane that would make a newcomer think that Queensland was a place of nothing but pushing, striving, green sugar under a blue bowl of sky.

There was a silky breeze blowing. Sophie told Garrick that up here the air was always silk. The small wind set the cane rolling in soft undulations of purple grey.

"Now do you agree?" she persisted.

"Agree?"

"That cane is lovely."

He did not answer at all this time, and Sophie set her chin stubbornly and determined to give him a lesson about cane.

"Around this district the cane reaches fourteen feet, Headmaster. Not very tall compared to New Guinea's twenty, but we have the highest sugar content in the world.

"This field is fallowing. It's terra-cotta red soil up here, and seen from a mountain top in varying stages of growth, with tramlines cutting it up into squares and rectangles, it all becomes a coloured mosaic.

"This cane now is grown from setts, or cuttings, and is called plant cane. The new crop from it will be ratoon cane. It will have a lower sugar content than the bigger grass, and give a lower yield per acre, but it saves a lot of expense."

"You know a lot about cane," Garrick Saxby said at last.

"I've lived in the north nearly all my life," she explained.

"I thought it might be since you had a sweet tooth."

"You don't like it, do you?" she deduced. "You don't see beauty in it. Some do, some don't."

"Just now I'm seeing sadness in it," he said abruptly.

"Sadness?" she queried.

"The family we're going to visit have lost their man through it, Miss Arthur. Cane treated them well. It maintained their little unit. But it also" . . . he paused . . . "took away the breadwinner."

"You mean—"

"Hans Scheerer . . . yes, he was Dutch, rather unusual, I'm told, since most of the sugar population is Italian—"

"Yes, it is."

"—died very tragically three days ago."

"I think," came in Sophie softly, "I know about it. I think I read it."

"All so unnecessary . . . such a waste," Garrick said, and sighed.

"The schoolmaster of the State school who contacted me said that Hans was held up for his turn with the mechanical harvester, so he began a manual cut himself. Some can cut, it seems, but some can't. Hans was no canecutter."

"I know," nodded Sophie, "I've seen it so often. It was all cut by hand when I was a child on holiday up here. I'll always remember it . . . the deep swathes going to and fro across the field and always the cane lying crosswise to the cut."

"Only," came in Garrick, "the deep swathe slipped, and Hans . . ."

He did not finish.

They came to Heathfell in the afternoon and checked in at the motel. Garrick gave Sophie half an hour to freshen up, then they started down a twisting track through tall cane to the adjoining small town of Sugar Hills.

"What is it we have to do?" Sophie asked.

"Take two out of five off a mother's hands. It won't be charity—they're all, according to the State school report, exceptionally bright."

"Have you any ideas, Garrick?" In her emotion Sophie was unaware she called him that and not Headmaster, or Mr. Saxby.

"Not the eldest, I expect," he said a little wearily, "since the mother will need him. Not the youngest since the mother will need that one, too, for a different reason."

"Two out of three," sighed Sophie now.

"Yes."

They had come to the end of the lane to a small house reaching barely higher than the completely encircling cane.

"It's going to be hard," Garrick said, "perhaps the hardest thing I've ever done." He paused. "Please help me, Sophie."

He pulled up the car and they got out.

It was the first time this big self-sufficient man had ever spoken to her like that, thought Sophie, as she followed Garrick Saxby up a neat bricked path. She bit her lip; it was all she could do not to run and touch his arm and say: "I'm with you, Garrick." But that would have been fatal. This man needed no one, not even, Sophie judged, his cousin Eve. He wanted to marry Eve, yes, but his reasons would never be so impulsive, so naïve, so emotional and basic as needing someone. Glad she had not acted on impulse, she stood silently beside Garrick as he clanged an old-fashioned knocker, a charming little piece that Sophie guessed must have been brought out from Holland.

The door was opening. A pale-faced woman tried to smile a welcome to them . . . but had to turn away. This time Sophie did obey her impulse, she went and put her arm around Mrs. Scheerer . . . she knew it would be Mrs. Scheerer.

"Please to come in," said the Dutch woman. "I will make tea."

Sophie went to offer her help, but Garrick shook his head the slightest degree. Seeing the wisdom of keeping Mrs. Scheerer occupied, Sophie went and sat in the parlour with the Headmaster. Parlour it indeed was, she thought, looking around her, it was one of those rooms most people have forgotten today. Its bare floors, polished lovingly to coax out the lights of the Queensland tallow-wood, was the only Australian touch. For the rest the room . . . the parlour . . . was purely Dutch.

There were five good pieces of Delft on the mantel-piece, and Mrs. Scheerer, coming in with the tea and noticing Sophie's eyes on the Delft, said: "One for each of the small ones for remembrance. Do you say that? For remembrance?"

"We say that, Mrs. Scheerer," nodded Garrick Saxby.

They talked on anything but what was on their minds at first. The weather . . . yes, said Mrs. Scheerer, she had found it hot in the beginning in Queensland, but she had been a young woman, and the young soon get used to things.

"It is when you are older that you no longer find yourself able to accept."

"Some things are hard to accept at any age," said Sophie gently.

"Yes." Then the floodgates broke.

". . . This terrible happening . . . This awful thing . . . He was so kind a man . . . Not strong enough for this kind of life, but the cane was good to us, and Hans made enough to have the crop cut." There were some minutes of crying.

"And it would have been cut again, only this time there was a delay, and Hans, poor Hans—" Again Mrs. Scheerer turned away.

When she was able to turn back, Mrs. Scheerer said: "Everyone has been so good, they are kind people."

"You have been good for their country, I think," said Sophie, "but now would you like to go home to Holland, Mrs. Scheerer?"

"Yes. But for the children this country is home. They were all born here, you see. But I would have liked to have gone back before—"

She did not finish that.

There was a noise somewhere along the track, and Mrs. Scheerer said: "The small ones are coming. They travel to school in the school bus. They do well at the school because although it is only a small school it is a good school, but Mr. Turner, the head teacher, says it is because they are bright. That I will believe. Hans was bright."

The clamour came closer. The door opened. Five little steps and stairs trooped in.

"Three boys, two girls, you see," Mrs. Scheerer smiled. "They have Australian names, though I do not know if Thomas, John, Dorothy, Robert and Jean go rightly with Scheerer."

"I think they do," said Sophie, watching the mother instinctively reach out for the youngest . . . look for help from the eldest. It was going to be as Garrick said.

"Miss Arthur here is very interested in cane, Thomas," said Garrick Saxby, "she would very much like to know all about it. Perhaps you children could tell her and show her."

A little surprised, since it had been the headmaster who had known nothing about the crop, Sophie rose and went outside with the children.

Sophie at once earned high marks with the young Scheerers for not leaping skyward when a sugar toad, some six inches in height, jumped past her.

Thomas told her gravely things she already knew, how the toad had been brought over from Hawaii to eat the cane beetle and now the cane farmers wanted something to eat the toad.

"My father would have thought it out," Thomas said. "He was a very clever man. But a book man, you must understand, he should never have cut cane."

"And you, Thomas? What do you want to be?"

"I like books," said Thomas sadly, and the resignation from so small a boy tugged at Sophie, "but my mother will need me."

Sophie had no answer to that. She was glad to see Garrick at the door of the cottage beckoning her.

"I think we should go now and fix up our lodgings for the night," he said.

"But we already—" Sophie recovered herself, and said that yes, they must do that.

They got into the car and went back down the track.

For two people who were so mututally moved over something, so concerned, so anxious to help, it was strange how neither of them spoke on the way back to the motel. A hundred things rushed to Sophie's lips, but she could not bring herself to say them. When she looked at Garrick, she saw he would not have listened, nor heard, he was deep in his own thoughts, and, judging by the tug to his mouth, they were sad thoughts.

They were sitting at dinner when the proprietor drew their attention to a red glow in the sky.

"Burning-off?" asked Garrick. He had been told by Sophie on the way up how all sugar cane has a lot of unusable rubbish that had to be got rid of.

The proprietor did not answer for a moment.

"It looks more than that," he said presently. "Cane flames up, but these flares are getting more than sugar to help them along, I'd say."

Garrick pushed his plate aside. Not knowing why she did so, Sophie followed suit. They both went outside.

"What are you thinking about?" Sophie asked the man.

"The Scheerers."

"But—"

"When you went out with the children this afternoon—"

"You mean when you got rid of me."

"Perhaps I did—well, then Mrs. Scheerer asked me something."

"Yes?"

"She asked could I take the *five.*"

"Five scholarships?"

"Yes. I told her no. Or at least I said how could I? I also asked her how she could manage without them, and she answered that she would be going, anyway. Going soon."

"Going? Going soon?"

"She's ill, Sophie. Very ill. There's a prognosis ni
She's quite calm about it, even, when she talks abou
her Hans, a little glad. But when she spoke of th
children—"

"Is there no one back in Holland? She mentione
home."

"No one. The home part was the country itsel
its people, but not her own people, nor Hans's peopl
for they have all gone."

"Why are you telling me this now? Why—why ar
you so concerned?"

"Because although I don't know this district I fee
that where we went this afternoon was—" He coul
not speak for a while. "I think," he managed at last
"it was there." He nodded to the red flare.

They sat up that night waiting for news. The host
seeing their anxiety, got busy on the phone, but it wa
not until after midnight that they learned the truth.

It *had* been more than cane feeding that viciou
flare in the sky, even though a spark from an adjacen
burning could have started the fatal flame, it had bee
the Scheerer house.

A timber house, dependent on tanks, surrounded b
dry cane. No wonder that the place had gone u
almost in minutes.

"Loss of life?" Garrick asked quietly.

"Yes," the motel proprietor said.

"How many?"

"Only one—the mother. The rest, the children
weren't in the house, they had been sent to a neigh
bour's for something. Out there a neighbour means a
least a mile."

"Are they being looked after now?" broke in Sophi
urgently. "The children are?"

"Oh, yes, you can be reassured about that."

But, outside in the garden again, Sophie wondere

if Garrick Saxby would ever be reassured about anything any more. He stood there in utter wretchedness, in deep pain. She knew he was experiencing the height and depth of despair.

"I know," she whispered, "I know, it's like an amputation."

"An amputation of love," he nodded. "She loved them. Now she's cut off."

Instinctively Sophie put her arm round the big man, and at once his head rested on her shoulder.

There were things she should have said, but all Sophie could think was: I wonder what happened to the five pieces of Delft.

They took the Scheerer children back with them the next day.

There was not a neighbour who did not come forward to ask to have one, or two, or even all of them, Mrs. Scheerer had been right when she had said " . . . they are kind people . . ." but when Garrick Saxby had pointed out that such bright little brains as the five possessed would be doing his school a good turn, they proudly agreed. Yes, they said, all the children were very clever, it was only right that they had their chance.

While the different families who had taken them in for the night gathered their pitiful belongings, Sophie said: "How can we fit them in, Headmaster? I mean, at Apa-Kingsley, I know that the waiting list is several years for the girls, more than that for the boys."

"There is always room kept for scholarship children, they are our gratuity, not the school theirs."

"But five?"

"It will be done. For the moment I'll put them in my Isle of Capri house until classes and dormitories are decided on. I would have done so, anyway, these children have had a terrible experience."

"How are they?" Sophie had not actually seen them yet today.

"Just numb, I would say. In a way that's good, it means we'll drive down with a minimum of trouble. It will be a miserable, wretched return, but I anticipate no worries."

"Was it a cane fire spark?"

"Probably. Had Hans been alive he would have been alerted and been able to save the house. Even Mrs. Scheerer might have been able to do something had she not been in the state she was. The children were asleep."

"Asleep? But—"

"According to Thomas, she roused them, said they would all go at once to the safety of a neighbour's."

"Yes?"

"Then, according to Thomas, as soon as they got out of the cottage she placed the responsibility on him of getting the others across the fields while she went back for something. He believed she was following at once, so did what he was told."

"Only she didn't come?"

"She just went back," Garrick said with difficulty.

"Why?"

"I suppose I could say for five pieces of Delft . . . for remembrance."

"Are you saying that?"

"Yes."

"Thinking that?"

"She was a wonderful mother," said Garrick abruptly, "and she knew she hadn't long, anyhow, so in this way—"

"The children were safe?"

"Yes."

"And they will be, Garrick? I don't mean just now, but later—later when all the sorrow and pity has worn off?"

"What do you think?" he answered warmly.

Presently he said: "Yes, we won't bother them with lessons this term. They'll stay on the coast. You must go down often . . . in fact you could go and live there."

"How could I, with my classes?"

"My dear Miss Arthur, the way you say that anyone would think you were not expendable."

"You really mean anyone would think I was a proper teacher," Sophie said bitterly.

"Even they are expendable," he shrugged, "though an unqualified one even more so."

"All the same, I won't go down. I mean not to stay. You must remember I have Father."

"Yes." He said it no differently than usual, except perhaps for a slight hesitation, but something in his voice sent Sophie's glance raking his.

"Sophie—" he said, but he said no more. The children were coming down the track.

They put them in the car. Two boys in front with Garrick, a boy and two girls in the back with Sophie. It was a squeeze, but their small worldly belongings fitted easily in the car boot.

It was even worse a journey than Garrick Saxby had said. Sophie tried a variety of I Spy games, but met with little response. Garrick did not get any help in his 'spot which car' contest. They had tea at an attractive roadhouse, but though Sophie carefully selected the things children like . . . peanut butter sandwiches, small iced cakes, icecream, the plates barely were touched.

Around dusk both Sophie and Garrick gave up trying any more, and they drove into a darkling night in silence. All the gay lights were flickering as they reached the Surfer's Golden Mile, but the children, though still wide-eyed, could not be diverted by the fairy glow.

"I also rang Mrs. Clayton," said Garrick, turning into the Isle of Capri bridge, "she'll have everything ready. Ready, too" . . . he gave her a quick sidewise look . . . "for you."

"No, Headmaster, I'll come often, but I have Father." This time Sophie looked full at him, challenging him to speak, but either the traffic was heavy or he had lost the urge, for he just kept going until they reached his island house.

Sophie helped Mrs. Clayton put the girls to bed while Garrick took over the boys. There was no trouble. The children were practically asleep on their feet.

They waited there until Mrs. Clayton reported cheerfully that even a pop band wouldn't have wakened them, then went back to the car for their last leg home.

The journey was entirely in silence. Apart from having nothing left in her to say, Sophie felt depleted. She knew when she got out that, like the children, she would be asleep on her feet.

But it turned out differently. The moment they pulled up Marion Javes, and a few more of the staff, came out on the verandah.

Marion's first words were solicitous ones for the children, but even in her exhaustion Sohpie noticed an excitement in the teacher.

"We took them to the coast until we can find room here for them," Sophie explained, noting, though abstractedly, Garrick disappearing into the office with Father.

"Well, there'll be room for *one,* anyway," Marion

announced. "We're one less since you left, Sophie."

"Yes?"

"Virginia," said Marion hurriedly now, obviously not wanting anyone to beat her to it, "has gone. She wasn't in her dormitory yesterday morning, and she hasn't been seen since."

CHAPTER EIGHT

"Gone?" Sophie looked incredulously at Marion Javes. "But where?"

"If we knew where," snapped Marion, and Sophie guessed that the strain was telling on the senior mistress, "we wouldn't be worrying you both now, not after all you've gone through. But we've done everything, tried everything, and the wretched girl has disappeared completely."

"But she was one of our best pupils."

"You know what I meant," said Marion, wretched herself, "when I said wretched."

"Yes, dear," placated Sophie sympathetically. She asked sinkingly : "Any of the boys missing?"

"No, and thank heaven at least for that. I mean, apart from the expected implication, with none of them gone, we have only one to look for. Oh, Sophie, where on earth can Virginia be?"

"Start from the beginning. When was her absence first noticed?"

"That's a very unfortunate point. No one knew until late this afternoon."

"But her room-mates?"

"You know Virginia, always studying—that is, she was always studying until these last few weeks. A change came over her then. She seemed to go stale on learning. Students often do. I recall May Perriman reporting her essays as having lost all their verve."

"Yes." Sophie was thinking of something else said

by someone else.—Said by Eve. 'I think,' Eve Saxby had said, and everyone—and Garrick Saxby—had dismissed it—'she could be in love.'"

Sophie begged Marion to go on.

"Virginia was more often than not in bed *after* the other girls in the room were asleep, more often than not up and down in the library again *before* they woke up. That is" . . . Marion repeated herself . . . "until the last few weeks."

"Her bed would have been unslept in this morning," pointed out Sophie practically, "so it should have been found out before this evening."

"Virginia's bed was always neat. She made it first thing, and never failed. You could say she was a perfect girl in every way, and now—"

"We'll find her," Sophie promised, trying to prevent Marion's tears that seemed ready to flow. She asked: "How far has the school searched, Marion?"

"As much as could be fitted in the several hours after we made the discovery and now."

"Has the family been told?"

"We agreed to let Headmaster decide on that."

"The police?"

"Another decision for Mr. Saxby, poor fellow."

"But the rest of the staff have been searching?"

"Searching high and low."

"And far?"

"Not far yet," admitted Marion Javes. "You see, the one who would have been the best help, being younger and stronger and more agile, unhappily had to be away."

"Bill Bethel?"

"Yes. It was his stand-down. Things always happen at the wrong time." She sighed.

Sophie nodded. Her brain seemed to be stretching out in ten different ways at the same moment. Bill

Bethel absent.—Eve too? she wondered. But she dared not ask.

"I'll see Mr. Saxby," she said.

Marion nodded, for the first time without words. The senior mistress turned back to the group of teachers, and Sophie heard one of them murmuring something about tea. She hoped they carried that out. They looked a very discouraged staff.

She went along to the office and tapped on the door.

"Come in," Garrick Saxby called.

When she entered she saw that Father had left, and Garrick, noting her inquiring look, told her he had ordered him to bed.

"Thank you," Sophie said. It was the first time, had she been in a reflective mood, that Sophie had thanked the headmaster for issuing an order that affected her father.

"You know our dilemma, of course?" he said.

"Yes."

"We won't go into it, Sophie, the pros and cons, the post-mortems, the over-study, the under-study, the what-have-yous, but what we will do, must do, is get that girl back."

"How?" Sophie despaired.

"You're a woman."—At any other time Sophie would have retorted that as far as he was concerned she was still a troublesome child, but this was not any other time.

"Yes," she conceded, "but I had little to do with Virginia. She was a brain, and as such totally uninterested in brawn. I didn't mean that as a pun," Sophie added.

"No, I think you mean that you and Virginia did not communicate much over physical jerks."

"I do, Headmaster."

"Her work has been going off—that's nothing. Virginia was fully prepared for any exam three months ago and would have been . . . *will be* . . . still fully prepared in three months' time. Just now there is a temporary and perfectly normal ebb."

"I hope that's right," burst in Sophie, "that *will be,* I mean, that *temporary.*"

"I hope so, too," he said gravely.

A few minutes went by.

"How exhausted are you, Sophie Arthur?" Garrick Saxby asked her directly.

"Curiously . . . now . . . not at all. Anyway, I couldn't go to bed. I mean, not knowing, as I don't know now."

"I couldn't, anyway," he shrugged. "It would have to be an all-night session regardless. *Virginia must be found.*" A pause. "But, my God, where?" He looked at Sophie. "Think. Think!"

"I am."

"Think back to when you were seventeen."

"I am trying, but I wasn't a brain, and never stale through over-study."

"But what were your thoughts, Sophie? Tell me. Help me. Did you want to travel the world? Go on the stage? Become a diplomat? Be a nurse? Fall in love?"

"The last two are getting hotter," admitted Sophie, no thought of deceiving him now.

"The nursing and the lover?"

"Yes. All seventeen-year-old girls see themselves in nursing uniforms and marrying a doctor."

"And failing a doctor?"

"Well—someone out of knee socks and this side of a hearing aid." Sophie smiled wanly.

"Which," he asked keenly, "would you put first? No, not the socks or the hearing aid, but which of nursing or romance?"

"Well—men," admitted Sophie honestly, "though I scarcely think that Virginia—"

"We'll rule out the male staff," he said sharply. "None of them are up to hearing aids, admittedly but they're still a bit long in the tooth for sweet seventeen."

". . . Bill Bethel?"

"*He* is ruled out, full stop," Garrick Saxby said shortly, and left it at that.

"No boy is missing," he went on before she could ask any questions regarding Bill Bethel, even look inquiring. "We've cross-examined a few of Virginia's age group and they can suggest nothing. No budding romance there. Sophie, did you only contact Virginia at phys ed?"

"Oh, no, she came voluntarily to my nature study classes, voluntarily since she couldn't take Botany for her exam without the help of a qualified teacher, and if you remember, Headmaster, I'm not that." Sophie stopped abruptly, a little frightened by the anger in his face.

"We're not here to discuss that," he said. "Have you no sense of timing? A girl is lost and you rake up a fire!"

"Yes. I'm sorry."

"Then go on."

"Virginia came to my classes, and as usual with Virginia was well ahead of the rest in no time. So much so that—Oh!" Sophie put her hand to her mouth.

"Yes, Miss Arthur?"

"So much so," said Sophie miserably, "that whenever Jim came over, she would seek him out to be told about layout, soil building, herbaceous plants, perennials, annuals, the rest."

"Jim is—?"

"Our supply gardener's boy."

"Boy?" he queried.

"No more than eighteen, or nineteen . . . oh, I don't know."

"But definitely past knee socks and not up to hearing aids?"

"Yes, but you can't think—"

"Oh, yes, Sophie, I can think all right. What's he like, this Jim? Tall, dark and handsome?"

"Medium, gingery and rather ordinary."

"Can you get closer than that?"

"Basin-cropped hair. It stands out. All the boys have long thick mops now . . . even our own boys are rather gollywoggish."

"But Jim is basin-cropped, you say. What exactly is that?"

"Straight round the bottom and a straight fringe. Rather like Sir Galahad . . . Sir Lancelot . . . any of the knights." Sophie finished: "Oh!" and clapped her hand to her mouth again.

"Sir Lancelot," nodded Garrick, "to Virginia's Guinevere."

"Perhaps she saw Jim as Galahad," hoped Sophie. "My good blade carves the casques of men, my tough lance thrusteth sure."

"My strength is as the strength of ten, because my heart is pure. Just hope on that, Sophie. Pray on it." Garrick was getting to his feet, pulling Sophie up after him. "Come on."

"Where are we going?" she asked.

"To check on Jim. Does he live in the mountains?"

"He lives with the Leylands who have the nursery. He's a kind of relation."

"It couldn't be better, then, that is if it had to be at all."

159

"Wouldn't it be wiser to phone?" Sophie suggested.

"What could I say?"

"You have overseas visitors . . . they very much like the bignonia tweediana—"

"What in betsy is that?"

"Our creeper over the fence."

"Oh."

"And they would like some but have to leave at once and could the boy—"

"I get you." He picked up the phone.

Whatever Mr. Leyland thought of being disturbed at such an hour for a root of the vine that grew over the fence. Sophie was not told, but she was informed some grave minutes later, phone down now, that much as he would have liked to have obliged, Jim was having his usual few days off. Good lad, Jim, he worked for days on end, then took his due in one mouthful, you could say.

"I quote Leyland," Garrick Saxby reported.

"What other quotes?"

"Jim went in the utility. The Leylands are quite pleased about that. When a boy gives his best, as Jim has, it's only fair to give him a few extras."

"Like the ute."

"For a few days," nodded Garrick. He paused. "And nights," he added. He sat down again, put his head in his hands.

As is always the case with women, Sophie at once grew strong.

"Well, what are we waiting for?" she snapped deliberately.

"Not for an inspiration, I can assure you. Sophie, I just don't know what to do."

"Then I'll tell you. You'll take up your keys from the desk, then the two of us will go down to the car."

"Then where?"

That stopped her. "I don't know," she admitted, "but we'll do that at least." She dabbed nervously at a tear, and the way it was with men with women who are weak, he recovered fully, took her arm and impelled her out and down.

They did not speak until he had driven the car out of the school drive then half way down the mountain. There he found a ramp for descenders finding themselves in trouble, and quickly occupied it.

"If anyone sees us they'll think we're lovers," he told Sophie, "not looking for lovers. All right, smarty, any ideas?"

She let that pass; he was, she knew, as thick with concern as she was.

"I have been thinking about that other dream of youth's long long dreams," she told Garrick. "The nursing one. Presuming these two ran away together" . . . she bit her lip . . . "they have to live, don't they? Virginia would have extremely little, Honor was very adamant about pocket money and to date you haven't changed it. She could not possibly have saved more than several dollars, and even that few is questionable. She spent every cent she could get hold of on books."

"Good reasoning, Sophie. I'll contribute something about Jim. When Mr. Leyland rationalized his lending of the nursery ute to Jim, the reason was Jim's small wage. Jim is learning the business, you see, not simply being employed."

"So," said Sophie, "they couldn't have got far. Petrol and all that."

"Fact established, but it doesn't help us much, does it?" Garrick glanced around him. "These mountains could hide armies. Then down on the Golden Mile there are so many rooms, digs, overnight lodgings behind the glittering lights that the job would be hopeless."

"They would have to have money," Sophie argued. "They could get none up here, but they could down there. Jim could get a job in a filling station in a twinkling, Virginia—"

"Yes? Virginia?"

"The Lady with the Lamp," Sophie said.

"Sophie, are you—"

"No, I'm not mad. I just think I know where Virginia would apply. Most girls apply. I mean girls of seventeen."

"Nursing?"

"Yes. There are two large hospitals, a few cottage hospitals. It could" . . . at a look on his face . . . "be a much more formidable list."

"I suppose you could be right."

"I am right," Sophie said with conviction. "We'll try the District first."

It came out exactly like that. The District, too, was a good primary choice.—Only one thing was wrong. Virginia had been there, in fact had finished her rostered time there . . . yes, that was prior to today . . . but she had not turned up since. It was like that with a lot of the young girls these times, they blew hot, then they blew cold, they—

"Not here." Sophie and Garrick turned away.

"Are you going to try all the filling stations?" Sophie asked flatly, as, side by side, they walked disconsolately back to the car. It was now well past midnight, but on the Gold Coast that was the time when life was lived. From now until dawn the lights would be glittering.

"No," said Garrick.

"Then?"

"Don't beggar me. I think we'll just get in and drive for a while."

They did all the islands . . . Chevron, Paradise,

Capri . . . then they turned west at Broadbeach and took the back way up the hills. They were still on the lower footlings when a car, coming towards them, took a bend much too quickly at the same time as some stray cattle chose to cross to the other side. Instinctively Garrick tried to miss the beasts, but Sophie saw he would run out of space and time. There was a moment of suspense . . . curious how long a moment it seemed . . . then the bank they were rimming was running out and dipping instead of a slope.

Sophie could not have said whether she cried out; whether Garrick did. All she was aware of was a shiver, a shudder, then an abrupt halt.

She was bitterly aware, too, that the other car had gone blissfully, unknowingly on; that the door, her door, anyway, had been jammed so tight in the descent she could not open it.

She turned to ask Garrick about his door . . . then saw that he had passed out.

Sophie went through a few moments of terror. There was a thready wound on the side of his head and a thin weave of blood was coursing down his temple and across one cheek. He's gone . . . or he's going, she thought.

"Garrick," she called, "Garrick, don't . . . don't! Oh, Garrick darling! Garrick, my very darling." She was aware, yet at the same time oddly unaware, of speaking aloud. She meant what she said, she realized that, but the knowledge was not such a shock as knowing she had meant it, yet not acknowledged it, ever since she had known this man. I loved him, she knew, even that day when he sat on the wrong side, or so I considered, of the desk. And now he is dying.

"I'm not." She must have said so aloud, because, though he still sat slumped, he now looked across at her.

"You're concussed."

"No."

"You're wounded."

"No. Only a bump."

"It's bleeding," she insisted.

"So would you have bled if you'd connected with the rear vision mirror."

"But you were unconscious."

"Sophie, I was winded. A complete winding like I received when I contacted the front panel can knock the daylights out of you. Mine are knocked out now. I'm just going to sit here for a while."

"I can't get out," she told him, "my door is jammed."

"So what?"

"So can I climb over you?"

"No. Also: shut up." He closed his eyes, and she saw the white around his lips and obeyed. After all, she thought, at this time of morning . . . yes, it was morning now . . . in a wrecked car, there was very little they could do.

And they were his first words when he stirred some ten minutes later.

"I'm better now. Lungs acting again. But there's no hurry now, there's nothing we can do tonight."

"This morning," she corrected him.

"This morning," he acknowledged. "You agree that there's nothing to be done?"

"Yes. But—"

"But what do we do with ourselves? Well, we clamber out the back doors . . . yes, my door is jammed as well . . . walk up the embankment, then keep walking to the nearest telephone. With luck, though I think it's improbable, we may snare a lift."

"Then what?"

"We go home, snatch some rest . . . yes, Sophie, we

both must grab an hour at least . . . then"—wearily—
"start the machinery."

"You mean parents, police, all that?"

"All that," he nodded, and shut his eyes briefly
again.

Again she did not disturb him, but covertly, in the
darkness, whenever a moonray lit the scene, or a faint
star gleam, she studied his face.

"Well?" he asked her, eyes still closed.

"I . . . I wasn't . . . I mean what are you asking?"

"Well, what did you find, Sophia? A good honest
countenance or a sly rogue's look?"

"If you think I was looking at you—"

"I do think, and you were." He sat up straighter,
but still did not seem ready to leave.

"I wonder," he said, "if among all the things that
have happened tonight, like me you've also thought of
another thing."

"Another thing?"

"The absence of Bill Bethel."

"It was his stand-down."

"Also" . . . he ignored her explanation . . . "the
absence of my cousin's widow."

"Eve."

"She's the only cousin's widow I possess. Well, did
you, Sophie?"

"No, not precisely . . I mean, Marion did tell me
that they hadn't had the services of Bill, and why, and
I did wonder fleetingly about—"

"About Eve? Why she was not around helping as
well? How could she, my dear, being absent?"

"Was she?"

"Was. Is."

"It was a pity," said Sophie, "I think she had more
insight than any of your staff. That day we discussed
Virginia she said at once that it could be love."

"At seventeen!"

"At any age," Sophie said.

"Well, Eve isn't around to issue any more pearls of wisdom. Neither is Bethel around to do the running about that he should be doing instead of me. Two of them gone at the same moment. Tell me, Sophie, does that indicate anything to you?"

"Why should it?"

"Oh, for heaven's sake, stop playing the fool, stop hedging. *Does it*?"

Sophie remembered eyes meeting, hands brushing, smiles bridging a room.

"Yes," she said in a rush, but she could not stop herself, it had to come out. "Yes, it does, Garrick. Oh, poor you. Poor, poor you!"

A minute went by, perhaps it was less, perhaps it was more. Then Garrick Saxby said:

"Oh, for heaven's sake!"

She looked at him in confusion, then understood, or believed she understood. Her triteness, her "Poor you" had exasperated him. He was not that kind of man.

Then she heard him protesting in disbelief: "Don't tell me that that's what you thought."

"I thought *you* and *Eve*," she said frankly. "Who else, Headmaster? You're not blood cousins. You had her photo on your table. You've fallen over backwards safeguarding her. You even considered tying her up."

"Your words," he corrected.

"But you liked the idea."

"Of course I did," he came back, "anything to keep Eve down would have got a good reception from me. Do you know why?"

"Why?"

"Because——" he began, then waited for her to sit back, too, before he went on.

"Terence Saxby, Eve's husband, was my first cousin, my father's brother's son. My parents died tragically while I was quite young, and Uncle Robert and Aunt Ellen brought me up with Terry. My stepsister, my mother's daughter by a first marriage, and some years my senior, went to Mother's side.

"I loved my uncle and aunt, but I never cared about Terry. He did not resemble his parents in any way, they were entirely worthwhile, intrinsic, in Aunt Ellen's case utterly sweet as well. But either because he was their only child and they spoiled him, or he was a throwback somewhere, Terry evolved into a smug, bullying, self-satisfied, self-opinioned, objectionable boy . . . young man . . . man. Oh, I know you shouldn't speak ill of the dead, but that was Terry.

"I suspect his parents knew it, too, but they still left him all their rather considerable worldly belongings."

"None to you?"

"I never needed any more," Garrick shrugged, "my own parents had been more than well placed. It was not Terry's first marriage, that marriage with Eve, even though he was the same . . . tender? . . . age as I was. Eve was his third wife. I have no doubt that the failure of the two previous marriages was as much, or more, Terry's fault as the girls he chose, but it still remains that their acquisitiveness must have impressed itself on Uncle Robert and Aunt Ellen to such a degree that when Terry took upon himself a third wife they made it a condition that the money that they already had paid out to the other two would not be paid out in this third instance unless the marriage had existed three years. They went to great pains in the will. The solicitor handling their bequests was even instructed that in the unlikely event of Terry's death before those three years, the widow, Eve, must not marry before the time was up, or if she did she was to forfeit what the previous wives had gained."

"But Terry's own money? Wouldn't that go to Eve?"

"Terry's money? Terry had no money. As fast as Uncle allowed him any, for Terry never worked, he spent it. Oh, no, there was nothing to come from my cousin."

There was silence for a few minutes. Sophie saw Garrick close his eyes, then open them again.

"After my aunt's and uncle's deaths . . . in about the same tragic circumstances as my own parents . . . I met Eve, and I knew at once if those two good people had met *this* one, not just heard of her from Terry as they had, they would not have penalised Eve. Admittedly she was immature, feathery, quite adorably silly in a way, but she was no gold-digger like Claudia and Kay had been.

"I saw her possibilities. I saw her worth. She was young and foolish and quite a little dumb, actually, but if my cousin Terry had gone even a little way her way, put one foot forward, she would have made him a wonderful wife. Made a good mother, too. You must know how she adores children."

"Oh, yes, I know."

"But even they were denied her," Garrick said.

"Then why did your cousin marry her?"

"She was . . . is . . . beautiful. You know that, too. It pleased Terry. In the circles he mixed he always had to have the best. She was a feather in his cap when he took her to his rich clubs, but once he had showed her off, he disregarded her.

"Then what I said seemed an unlikely event happened. Terry quite unexpectedly died. Too hectic a life, no doubt. Just as unexpected was the executor role I had imposed on me."

168

"From Terry?"

"No. I told you, he had nothing. No, from Uncle Robert and Aunt Ellen. The marriage had to last three years before Eve could have any money."

"But it couldn't last with Terence dead."

"My uncle and aunt were of the old school. They truly believed marriages were made, and accounted for, in heaven. Anyway" . . . impatiently . . . "they made it a separate clause. They said that there was nothing at all to come in that unlikely event . . . Terry's death, I mean . . . should Eve marry again in three years."

"How long is it since—"

"Since Terry died? Two years, two months. I think . . . yes, I very much think, Sophie Arthur, that Eve has jumped the gun by ten months."

"Unless—"

"Unless?"

"Unless they've just gone off together," blurted Sophie.

"Or unless they haven't gone off together at all. Who knows yet?"

"Who knows?" agreed Sophie . . . and suddenly she was thinking of the younger actor and actress in this scene, thinking of Jim and Virginia.

Garrick must have been thinking in the same strain. A little abruptly he said: "All right, I'm recovered now. Just as well, for I'm going to need some muscle on this window . . ."

He pushed . . . Sophie helped him, and presently the window opened. They tumbled out and climbed up the embankment.

They were lucky. Even at such an impossible time of night . . . or morning . . . they were picked up, and the driver was not only going into town but out of town again and out to the hinterland. Yes, he knew the Apa School, he nodded. Hadn't it recently become co-ed? He felt sure he had read somewhere that it had become co-ed.

"It has indeed," said Garrick, and he looked wryly at Sophie. So much had happened, his look said, since Apa had become Apa-Kingsley.

It was not far from piccaninny daylight when they walked through the gates and down the drive to the school. Neither of them spoke, except for Garrick's resigned :

"Oh, well, tomorrow is another day."

Sophie stopped herself from reminding him that tomorrow, the tomorrow he was apparently referring to was today already.

She dragged herself into the house, across to the stairs . . . then stopped at Garrick's arm on her arm. She followed behind him as he nodded to the kitchen.

There, standing at the stove, was Virginia. She was cooking an egg.

"Virginia!" they both said together, and Virginia turned round to them, though not quick enough to prevent some fat tears falling into the pan.

"I was hungry," she said.

"I was hungry." Of all the people cooking eggs in the kitchen at four in the morning, Virginia was the last person Sophie could have expected; of all the things she had expected Virginia to say when . . . if . . . they found her, was :

"I was hungry."

"Of course, darling." She stepped eagerly towards Virginia. "Now sit down and rest, because I'm going to fix you a really good break—"

"Afterwards," came in Garrick Saxby firmly. "*Afterwards*." He waited to let that sink in. "After, not before, we iron all this out. Do you hear me, Miss Arthur?"

"But we have hours yet before Cooky comes down."

"Later. I haven't the least fear that Virginia is dying on her feet for sustenance. I may be wrong, but I think there've been a few snacks of fish and chips since she left Apa."

"Hamburgers," sighed Virginia.

"So waiting a little longer won't kill her. Indeed, with everything out and aired, I think it will improve her appetite. Do you agree, Virginia?"

"Oh, yes," said Virginia, tears welling again, "I wouldn't have enjoyed it all choked up like I am now. Thank you, Headmaster."

Sophie did not thank him, she felt he was being very hard. "At least," she appealed, "can I make coffee?"

"Yes, since I, too, could do with some coffee. Bring it to the study, Miss Arthur. Come along, Virginia." He went off with the girl.

Never had Sophie brewed coffee quicker; she did not trust that man, he could be browbeating the girl.

But when she kicked on the office door with her foot because she couldn't turn the handle with a tray in her hands, and he opened up, Virginia was reading one of the text books set for her exams.

"I never thought," she said tremulously, "I could miss this so much."

"The written word," nodded Garrick.

"Yes." Virginia looked gratefully at Sophie with the coffee. "Thank you, Miss Arthur. We couldn't afford anything to drink, only to eat—coffee is twenty-five cents a cup, did you know?" She must have remembered what was to come after the coffee, for she put her cup down into its saucer with a little clatter.

"Drink up, be like the condemned man," Garrick advised . . . and Virginia shed a tear, then actually giggled.

"I suppose I am like a condemned man," she said.

She finished her cup, and as Sophie replenished it, replenished all three, Garrick said:

"When did you run away, Virginia?"

"It's hard to think back now. I know it's not long ago really, but it seems like years."

"All the same, think."

"It was the night before last night."

"It's now another morning, remember."

"Then it was the night before the night before last night."

"She left," came in Sophie, "the night before the morning we went up to Sugar Hills."—That made three nights missing, Sophie thought, counting last night, and you had to count it, too, because obviously Virginia had arrived home only minutes before they had. Three nights to be accounted for. Her heart sank.

"What time, Virginia?" Garrick demanded.

"After dinner. I went down to the garden, it was a lovely evening, and Jim had just delivered some seedlings, and . . . well . . . we . . ."

"All prearranged, of course?"

"Oh, no, Headmaster, none of it."

"Oh, come, Virginia, don't take me for a fool. It was a beautiful evening and you go into the garden and see Jim and simply fade, like a Fitzpatrick travelogue, into the horizon."

"Headmaster, I don't understand," appealed Virginia.

"Of course she doesn't," fumed Sophie, "she's at least thirty years away from Fitzpatrick and travelogues. Why, even I can't remember."

"How nice to be so fresh and new," he said sarcastically. "Please, Miss Arthur, will you try to quell your youthful enthusiasms long enough for me to speak with Virginia. Well, Virginia, I'm waiting. Do you still wish to stick to that ridiculous story that nothing was planned?"

"Oh, yes, because it's true. Jim was putting slug pellets round the seedlings and he looked up and saw me and saw the night, I expect—"

"I expect."

"And said: 'Let's drive.' "

"And you replied?"

"I said: 'Oh, yes.' "

"But why, Virginia? Why did you say that? You knew you were not allowed out of the school grounds without permission."

"Yes, I knew, but I never even thought about it. I'd felt pretty fed-up for some time . . . I was ready for the exam at the beginning of the year, not the end . . . somehow things were stale, not bright and interesting any more. But a ride down the mountains with Jim promised something different. It was a lovely night, I told you, and Jim—well, Jim is really—I mean he's really—"

"Yes? Keep telling."

"About Jim? Or what happened?" asked Virginia a little warily.

"About what happened. We already know about Jim. Young Galahad, isn't he?"

"Oh, yes," Virginia said.

"Go on."

"We drove down the mountains. They were all citrusy from the wild limes, the scent seems to come out more at night. And the lights from the coast!"

"I know," nodded Garrick, "some of the high-rise penthouses seem to string stars around them. I swear one wears a moon as a brooch."

"Oh, Headmaster, you *know*!"

"I know. Keep on, Virginia."

"We talked . . . and talked. Jim told me how his

173

job often got him down. He loved the living things, but he didn't like lots of sidelines like delivering and mixing manure. I told him I'd gone stale on my work, that sometimes I felt that another session with Shakespeare would send me nuts .

"He said he often felt like doing something more—well, needful."

"Like?" asked Garrick.

"Being a doctor. He said he liked living things, so that must include people as well as plants."

"Generous of Jim."

"Oh, he is, he is. Then I said : 'What a coincidence, I would like to be a nurse.' " Briefly Garrick's eyes met Sophie's. "Then we got this beaut idea of working at a hospital."

"Not Jim as a doctor, surely," protested Garrick.

"No, as a handyman, but watching intently to establish to himself whether he would like medicine."

"Yes?"

"I would apply as an aide, or ward help."

"Tch-tch," said Garrick, avoiding Sophie's signals, "I thought a matron at least."

"You have to advance to that," Virginia explained.

"And did you advance? Either of you? I'm taking it that you were accepted."

"They rushed us. Not many will take on night work. We were started straight away."

"Go on."

There was a silence.

"Go on, Virginia."

"It was hard, Headmaster," admitted Virginia. "I never thought work would be so hard. I never stopped emptying, filling, fetching, taking away, measuring, pouring, changing and making beds all night."

"And Jim?" he asked.

"Jim had blisters like he's never had before, not

174

even grubbing out a tree." Virginia sighed. "All the same," she said proudly, "we lasted the night, and even went back the next night, so you can't say we didn't try."

"No," Garrick allowed.

Sophie said to herself: "Two nights out of three accounted for." She asked aloud in a calm voice that surprised even her:

"Where did you rest in the day?" She could not bring herself to say where did you sleep?

"On the beach. We both flaked out. We just lay there sound asleep all day in the sun. We got very burned."

"Then back to work?"

"Yes."

"Was it easier second go?"

"No," admitted Virginia, "it was harder. When we were finished in the morning we pooled our money and went into a cinema and slept there. We were too sore to lie on the beach again."

"That brings you to last night," Garrick announced.

"Yes." Virginia hung her head.

"I'm waiting, Virginia," said Garrick.

"I can't tell you."

"Darling, tell me," urged Sophie. "I want to help, but how can I unless I know?"

"You would be disappointed, Miss Arthur."

"Perhaps, but I think you would sooner we knew."

"Yes, I would, and I know Jim would, too. We . . . well, we never turned up at work. We got as far as the hospital, then Jim said 'I can't.' I said 'I can't, either.' We knew we were being weak, but we just couldn't. I was thinking about all that drudgery, that emptying, filling, changing, taking away, measuring, pouring, and Jim was thinking about more blisters. So—"

"So?"

"So we dropped out," said Virginia simply, "and came home."

"It took you a long time." Garrick's voice was sharp and probing. "You didn't get back until morning."

"The utility broke down," said Virginia, "and Jim had to fix it. He didn't mind, though, he likes doing constructive things like that."

"You didn't like it, though?"

"Oh, yes, I did, I felt much better in myself by then, I felt I had got over something."

"Got over Jim?"

"Jim?" Virginia looked surprised. "What do you mean 'got over Jim', Headmaster?"

"Was there anything to get over?" asked Garrick frankly. "You're seventeen, Virginia, and so near to a woman I can't talk to you as a child any more. *Was* Jim mending the truck all the time?"

"No, Headmaster."

"Then?"

"Once he came and sat in the cabin with me, and we talked about everything. We laughed at ourselves wanting to be a doctor and a nurse, because Jim really doesn't, and I don't. I know that now.

"We agreed you have times like these, times when you can't see the sense in things. Jim wants to create beautiful landscapes, but he couldn't see how delivering seedlings or putting snail pellets around or mixing manure would help, and I wanted to go to university, but I couldn't see how reading the same books over and over would help."

"But eventually you came to a compromise?"

"Yes."

"And then?"

"Jim went back to finish the truck."

There was a silence, then :

"Virginia, is that all?"

Virginia did not answer.

"*Virginia*!"

"No, Headmaster. Jim kissed me and I kissed him." Virginia paused. "Goodbye."

"Goodbye?"

"He's going on to agricultural college. I'll go . . . at least I hope I'll go . . . to university."

"You'll meet up again," broke in Sophie. She was unaware that tears swam in her eyes. "You both will graduate, and one day—"

"Miss Arthur." Garrick Saxby's voice cut in furiously. As Sophie's voice trailed off, he said acidly: "I think you must need sleep, you're certainly babbling some unusual things." He got up. "Bed, both of you. Unless you still want breakfast, Virginia?"

"No, I don't."

"Then bed. At once."

"Yes, Headmaster."

"Yes, Headmaster."

They went up together.

At the door of her dormitory, Virginia said: "Thank you, Miss Arthur."

"You should thank Mr. Saxby."

"Thank you for what you said about one day. Because— because I think that, too. So does Jim. Goodnight, Miss Arthur."

"It's good morning now, darling," Sophie said tenderly. She watched the girl go in. How sweet, how touchingly sweet is youth, what hopes they have, what dreams—

"I said *bed*," Garrick Saxby fairly boomed from the stairs, and Sophie went double-quick into the safety of Honor's suite.

CHAPTER NINE

Several things happened that month.

Jim left the Leyland Nursery to start at agricultural college.

"He was only ever sent here to be tried out," said Mr. Leyland. "My brother didn't want him put into something he might think he liked, then found he didn't. Well, Jim did like it, not all of it, naturally, not the mixing of the fertilizer—"

"The deliveries and the snail prevention pellets," put in Sophie unthinking. She happened to be there when Mr. Leyland made his own delivery now that Jim had left.

"Quite right, Miss Arthur, but most of it he took to straight away—the propagation, the experimental section, the cross-breeding. He's a natural, I'd say. In four years' time—"

"Is that how long his degree course will take?"

"Yes."

"As long as Virginia's B.A. and Dip.Ed."

"Miss Arthur," had come in Garrick Saxby, who had joined the small group listening to the nursery-man, "I believe you're on roster."

Sophie hadn't been on roster, she had known it, he had known it. But she had left.

The next thing to happen had been Virginia's exam. Virginia had come out of the examination room with a confident smile.

"Everything was what I wanted. There was nothing

178

I felt I couldn't handle. Even the essay pleased me, and I feel sure, without boasting, the examiners will be pleased, too. I felt all fresh and new, not a bit jaded as I was before. I think . . . oh, I'm keeping my fingers crossed, too . . . that I'll gain an entry."

Another thing was the happy inclusion of the five Scheerer orphans into Apa-Kingsley, the two girls into the Apa section, the three boys into the Kingsley. As each of the five had exceptional promise educationally, the school board had been eager to accept them.

"Just now we'll leave it at that," Garrick Saxby said. "What comes after school days can be resolved later on."

The children had remained on the coast until it had been considered they were sufficiently out of their shocked, numbed state to become what they essentially were once more, and that was small men and little women.

Eve had helped out there . . . and that was another thing that had happened. She and Bill had not returned directly to the school, but, at Garrick's suggestion . . . or order? . . . had gone instead to his Isle of Capri house. There they would play mother and father to the bereft five, and whom better for that role than a husband and wife? Yes, Eve and Bill had married.

As she had shown Sophie her ring, Eve had said: "Poor Garrick didn't want it like this. It wasn't that he didn't want Bill, he didn't want anybody, not for those three years. Something about money. As though I could care about money! Sophie, I have all my riches in Bill."

"Well, I know Bill has in you, Eve."

"I had a miserable life with Terry. I should never have married him, but I was young and flattered by the attentions of a mature, attractive man-about-town.

He never loved me, Sophie, he only ever wanted to show me off."

"Well, you are rather a dish, Eve."

"But Bill doesn't see me that way. Oh, I guess he thinks I'm all right to look at, I mean I would want him to think that, but I wouldn't want it to be the beginning and the end, Sophie. It isn't, and never will be, with Bill."

"You're happy, aren't you?" Sophie said almost with wonder. How do you get happy like that? she was despairing.

"Happy to heaven," Eve nodded. "And you? You and—" She must have seen a closed-up quality in Sophie's face, for she did not finish.

"Yes, happy, Sophie," she repeated.

The other thing that happened was—Father. Mr. Headmistress . . . somehow, as Marion Javes said afterwards, he would always be that . . . died peacefully one sweet spring morning. Sophie went into his room to waken him with a cup of tea as she always did, and Father had gone.

How long does it take for pain to sink in? For pain to really touch and hurt?

Sophie did not know. She only knew that she continued standing there looking at Father and holding the cup of tea until someone . . . Garrick Saxby . . . took the cup from her hand.

Then he took Sophie from the room.

She still did not feel pain . . . she did not feel anything really. She let the headmaster sit her down and give her a new hot cup of tea.

"For Mr. Headmistress's," he said gently, "would be too cold now for you to drink."

"You knew." Realization was beginning to flood into Sophie, numbness to retreat.

"Of course."

"Did the others know?"

"I think so. Yes."

"Then why was I left ignorant? Oh, Garrick, why was I guarded like that? Wrapped in cottonwool? Why was I not told?"

"I never wanted it so. I talked with Mr. Arthur about it many times. But he didn't seem to think you were ready."

"Ready?" she queried.

"To know."

"Was I such a child?" she cried.

"I don't know, Sophie, but he told me that he had tried to tell you several times."

"You mean he knew himself?"

"Oh, yes, my dear, he knew, why otherwise that 'cartilage'?" A fond little laugh.

"Father's knee . . . or leg . . . or whatever it was."

"Whatever it was is right, Sophie, for really it was nothing at all. When we came home that particular day, your father had just suffered an extremely grave and painful coronary."

"Then why didn't the others tell me?"

"They never saw it, they only found him on the floor, they only believed what he told them."

"About the newel post?"

"Yes. When the doctor came he was warned not to move around. But rather than take you into his confidence, Mr. Headmistress had his leg put into inactivity. With a trussed-up leg, you simply can't move around. What is more important, you have your reason not to."

"But why?" Sophie intoned again.

"Because he loved you, I expect. You have that effect on people, you know, of making them love you. Honor told me about it first of all, then when I met you I found out for myself."

"You've spoken of Honor before. Did you know her?"

"I should. She was my stepsister, a child of m' mother's earlier marriage. She was a grand person."

"What did she say about me?"

"That you were spoiled rotten," he grinned. "No not really, of course, but that your father doted on you, and no wonder. She's lovable, Garrick, were Honor's exact words, so consequently she's loved."

"What else?"

"She spoke of your obsession for your father, how you yearned for him to be Head."

"*You* put it down to my wanting to be Miss Head master," Sophie pointed out.

"Perhaps I was right, too," he shrugged. "How ever, that wasn't to be."

"Because of Honor's qualifications?"

"No, because even then your father knew it would not be very long for him. He could have been Head Honor could have got it for him, and would have, too only he told her his prognosis."

"Yet he never told me."

Garrick paid not attention to Sophie's cry. "So Honor agreed to go on," he said, "but Fate, as Fate often does, stepped in and took Honor first. *That* was unexpected." He sighed.

"Then you came?"

"Only temporarily. You know that. Schoolmastering is not my forte—education, yes, but I've never been tied to one school."

"It must have killed you," she said shortly.

"You're sounding a little better," Garrick Saxby smiled thinly, "more like yourself."

"Sour! Snappy!"

"Your words, Miss Arthur. No, it hasn't killed me, rather has it given me food for thought. I've always liked children as a whole, education as a whole, but neither of them individually nor close. Now—"

"Now?"

"I find my views changing. I find myself thinking not about schools, but school, not about staffs, but staff. I suppose you could say I've reached my peak and now I'm coming down."

"I wouldn't call it a descent but more a levelling. I think it would be a fine thing to be headmaster of a fine school, and Apa is a fine school."

"Apa-Kingsley."

"Apa-Kingsley," she agreed.

"Well, I think so, too, Sophie. Though I must give it more thought." He paused. "Will you?"

"Will I? But where do I come in? I'm not even qualified, you've been at pains ever since you came here to tell me that, so I and a fine school just don't go together."

She had risen. Now the pain was catching her up. She was feeling the amputation.

"Why?" she cried again. "Why? Why?"

"He tried to tell you," Garrick reminded her.

"Yes, I remember now. Once he said : 'Sophie' and waited for me to help him say more, only—only I didn't. Then once, coming back from the garden, he—he—"

Sophie could stand no more.

She turned and ran to her room.

The week ran out, a week of sorrow for the staff and the children as well as for Sophie. There had been no one at Apa, and very soon at Apa-Kingsley, who had not loved Mr. Headmistress.

"I'll always see him," said Marion Javes, "taking his class into the bush to find suitable bark for bark pictures, then leaves and roots from which to extract

183

his own colours to paint those pictures. Mr. Head
mistress is a loss."

"Yes, he is a loss," Sophie agreed.

Eve and Bill were living in Garrick's island house
on the coast. Being a phys ed teacher, Bill was no
called upon for individual duties as were the rest o
the staff, and Garrick told Sophie quite plainly that he
did not want Eve around.

"You didn't always say that," Sophie reminded
him.

"I had the responsibility of her then, now she i
Bill's bane."

"What a horrid alliteration!"

"It wasn't meant as unkindly as it sounds. It i
quite apt, though, isn't it? Bill's bane. Now what ca
I serve up for myself? Garrick's girl?" He looked
steadily at Sophie, so long and so steadily she looked
away.

"It would be hard to find an alliteration for Eve,"
she said conversationally.

"As far as Eve is concerned it's totally unsuitable."

"I don't think so."

"I do. Eve may look the eternal temptress but actu
ally she's a mother pure and simple. Born for tha
role, and may heaven bless her with many, but no
our kids up here, she'd have had them ruined had she
stayed on. I'm very glad to have my cousin-in-law a
far away as the coast."

"Will Bill be pleased commuting every day?"

"It's a lovely drive and no hardship," Garrick re
turned.

"Suppose you want your house, Headmaster?"

"I won't."

"You may decide to go back to the executive side o
education."

"I won't, but if that did happen I would be all ove

Australia as I've been before, so I still wouldn't require the canal place."

"You mean as your home?"

"Good heavens" . . . irritably . . . "why are you trying to pin me down like this? I'm staying here at Apa-Kingsley as Headmaster, Miss Arthur. I've found the work to my liking, the surroundings to my liking, the staff."

"Qualified, of course."

"Of course."

Sophie cleared her throat. Now was her moment to recite her resignation piece. She had been practising it for days.

"Headmaster," called one of the teachers along the corridor, "you've allowed me only one period on Wednesday afternoon, yet two on—"

Garrick bowed perfunctorily to Sophie, a bow that was also a dismissal.

Sophie watched throughout the day for another opportunity, but none came. After dinner, while Garrick chaired a staff meeting which, being unqualified, she was not required to attend, Sophie decided to pack her bags.

She had already bundled Father's clothes and sent them to a charity he had laughingly chosen once when they had sat at the window talking about . . . yet never really *reaching* . . . such final things. There were no school duties for her to attend to now, so she could act on something she had had in mind for some time regarding herself.

And this time, she thought as she worked, there would be no arguments over apartments. Glenda Morrison had two beds in her room, and when Sophie had told her she might be sharing with her temporarily Glenda had been most agreeable.

"I'm pleased to see that the Board is renovating at last," Glenda had said, taking it that Sophie was moving out while the painters or whatever moved in, and because it was easier like that, Sophie had not explained.

She clasped her bags now and teetered to the door. She turned the handle and tried to open the door, but someone stronger, also unimpeded with bags, was pushing the other way.

"What in tarnation—" said a voice.

"Oh, good evening, Headmaster."

He did not answer her greeting. "Where are you going with those bags? Doing a midnight flit?"

"It's not midnight, and generally such flits are done by people behind in their rent. That at least is not one of my sins."

"I'm glad you could find one instance," he allowed, and pushed again, pushed Sophie, and the bags back into the flat. "Where are you going?" he repeated.

"To Glenda Morrison's room. She has two beds."

"Good lord, why this sudden closer settlement?"

"Because I can't occupy a double suite when I'm single, can I? Besides—"

"Besides?"

"Besides for the reason that I'm going, Mr. Saxby. Resigning. Leaving. And leaving one room will be much simpler when the time comes than leaving a suite."

"Who says you're leaving?"

"There's nothing to stop me. As an unqualified teacher, a hanger-on you could say, I come under no award, no" . . . a deep breath . . . "rule."

"You really mean no authority."

She smiled blandly at him. "Exactly. Soon, very soon, I'll be as free as the wind."

"And you'll like that, won't you?"

"Yes, I believe I will."

"A pity for you then that you have to have other thoughts. Because, Miss Arthur, you are *not* resigning, you are *not* leaving, most of all you are *not* abandoning this suite, *not* being free as the wind."

She stared at him, but he afforded her no opportunity to interrupt.

"Instead" . . . he looked long at her, looked deeply, extractingly . . . "I'm moving in."

"But—"

"But is that a done thing in a school, you ask, even taking into consideration our now permissive age? No, Miss Arthur, I entirely agree. It is not. So we are— marrying first."

"Ma—" But he was holding up his hand.

"To put it as clear as I can for your muddled little head, also putting it briefly, I found you as Honor found you. Lovable . . . and so loved. Loved, in short, by me.

"You came bounding in one day to find me at the executive side of the desk, and that killed you, but oddly, it reincarnated me.

"I had become a piece of chalk, a school ruler, a primer, a blackboard, a piece of educational advice. I was a warning to some erring teacher, a word of encouragement to an uncertain one. Praise.

"But I wasn't breathing, seeing, hearing . . . feeling, Sophie, until *you* came in that day.

"I tried to dislike you. For all that Honor had said, I still thought of you as an ambitious girl. The only thing that did flummox me was your lack of ambition where *I* was concerned. You wanted to be Miss Headmaster if your father became Principal, already you were Miss Headmistress as Honor's stepdaughter, but you never cast envious eyes on—something else."

"Something else?"

He looked at her a long moment. Then:

"Mrs. Headmaster."

"Mrs. Headmaster? But—"

"Yes, Mrs. Headmaster. It's quite a coveted position in most schools I've inspected, and I've inspected many."

"Mrs. Headmaster . . ." Sophie repeated, almost as though she was tasting it. She looked up at him.

"Yes," he nodded. "But that would have entailed a certain happening, wouldn't it? Your marriage with the Headmaster?"

"Well—yes, it would."

"It would, and it still does. For I'm staying on here, Sophie Arthur, my theory days are over, my action days are beginning. Beginning in one minute, as it happens. In one minute I'm crossing over to you and taking you in my arms as you've never been taken before." A pause. "Or have you?"

"I haven't, but—"

"After that, you're placing the things in these bags back in this flat. After that you're helping me carry mine in."

"Before we . . . I mean . . . that is . . ."

"Before we marry? Say it, Sophie, say it loud and clear. No, my dear, after all, we are a school, and we have the young around us to be influenced in the right and accepted way.

"And the right and accepted way is to come downstairs now and tell the staff, show them this ring I took a risk in buying, then let me drive you down to the coast where you'll stay with Eve and Bill until we marry tomorrow morning."

"Tomorrow morning?" she gasped.

"Sophie, be reasonable. This is the best suite, you can't expect me to wait until you set a date."

"But you could come in now."

"I couldn't," he said truly . . . and she could *feel* the truth . . . "without you."

He took her hand and led her to the window to look down and out. Down at the night-silvered beaches of this south-east Queensland, at a moon rising out of the Pacific, at a penthouse borrowing a diadem of stars to wear on its top floor.

"I love you, Sophie Arthur," he said. "What can I do to have Sophie Arthur love me?"

"Love you or covet Mrs. Headmaster?" she asked frankly.

"Either will have to do," he accepted, "only don't let me know, just let me hope for the best."

"Then you have the best, Garrick, I'd love you even if you were unqualified," she half laughed, half cried as he pulled her triumphantly into his arms.

"I feel so carefree, so boyish with you, young Sophie," he revelled, "that I could be just that, a boy. But I'm not, I'm the Principal, and if that makes you the smallest bit happier, it makes me happier, too.

"So come along, darling, the staff are waiting, the school is waiting, everyone is waiting. I'm waiting.

"Waiting for our Mrs. Headmaster."

Me, marvelled Sophie. *Me*.

And went.

Harlequin

the unique monthly magazine packed with good things for Harlequin readers!

A Complete Harlequin Novel

You'll get hours of reading enjoyment from Harlequin fiction. Along with a variety of specially selected short stories, every issue of the magazine contains a complete romantic novel.

Readers' Page

A lively forum for exchanging news and views from Harlequin readers. If you would like to share your thoughts, we'd love to hear from you.

Arts and Crafts

Unusual handicraft articles are a fascinating feature of Harlequin magazine. You'll enjoy making your own gifts and indulging your creativity when you use these always clear and easy-to-follow instructions.

Author's Own Story . . .

Now, meet the very real people who create the romantic world of Harlequin! In these unusual author profiles a well-known author tells you her own personal story.

Harlequin Cookery

Temptingly delicious dishes, plain and fancy, from all over the world. Recreate these dishes from tested, detailed recipes, for your family and friends.

Faraway Places . . .

Whether it's to remind you of places you've enjoyed visiting, or to learn about places you're still hoping to see, you'll find the travel articles informative and interesting — and just perfect for armchair travelling.

Harlequin

An annual subscription to the magazine — 12 issues — costs just $9.00.
Look for the order form on the next page.

Don't miss your copy of North America's most exciting and enchanting magazine!

Subscribe now to the Harlequin Romance readers' own magazine . . . Harlequin . . . available only through Harlequin Reader Service 12 exciting editions for only $9.00